PAST DECEIVING

by

Michael Limmer

Wilt thou forgive that sin where I begun,
Which is my sin, though it were done before?
John Donne.

This is a work of fiction.

The characters are products of the author's imagination,

and any resemblances to persons living or dead

is entirely coincidental.

'Past Deceiving'

©Michael Limmer 2022

ISBN

PROLOGUE: London, 1943

As the staff car nosed into the busy London street, he saw the place immediately. "Pull in on the left," he ordered the driver. "Here, man, here."

The driver drew the car into the kerb.

"Wait here," he snapped. "I shan't be long."

"Very good, sir."

He swung his long limbs out on to the pavement and stood for a moment looking around, idly tapping the swagger stick against his thigh.

People bustling past appraised his uncompromising stance, the crisp uniform with the array of gleaming medals across his chest, the shoes polished to a high sheen. Some nudged their neighbour surreptitiously. "Looks like one of them War Office bigwigs. Dare say one of the chorus gals is his floosie." He ignored them all, indeed, hardly heard them. He was there for one purpose alone.

He strode up to the entrance. Two soldiers tumbled out, each with a girl on his arm. Recognising his rank with alarm, they saluted hastily and scurried away. But he paid them no attention.

He stood in the doorway, hands on hips, imperiously scanning the scene before him. The red neon sign above the door informed him that he was about to enter the Elysium Café, while a poster on a panel to the side proclaimed: *'Miss Valerie Kaye, South London's Lark, and her Larkettes, with Findlay Stratton and his Orchestra.'*

His lip curled in contempt. This was the time of war, and here before him stood a building crammed with people in various states of drunkenness, laughing, dancing and canoodling. What they were doing amounted to nothing short of a betrayal. There was a war to be fought and won, and they didn't seem to care! He burned with righteous anger, because they knew no shame.

The room was thick with people making an unholy noise. They ranged four or five deep along the bar, while away to the right, a small orchestra was tripping out an unbearably jolly tune, to which numerous couples gyrated languidly, their perspiring bodies melding together.

He spied his quarry almost immediately. Out of uniform, as might have been expected, never wasting an opportunity to disgrace his country. Typically, the boy lounged at the centre of the noisiest group, all of them in civvies, the painted women unashamedly flaunting their hateful bodies.

He marched over and planted himself before them, his face austere, his stance intimidating. It must have been a full minute before one of the women looked up and noticed him: the rest were busy laughing, joking and carousing.

"Here, Freddie. There's some old geezer glaring down at us. He don't look very happy."

He was glad to see the smile wiped off the boy's insolent face, as Freddie looked up sharply. A touch of guilt too, perhaps? He doubted it.

"Father – are you here to congratulate me? We're married, you know. And they've allowed me a few days' leave for my honeymoon. Good of them, eh? Forty-eight hours in smoky, bombed-out old London." He glanced busily around. "I should introduce you to her. Although, hang about, she'll be on in a minute..."

His voice trailed away before his father's face of thunder. Everyone whipped round in their seats, as the father began to rant and rave, condemning his son and the trollop he'd married.

"Everything you've ever done has been in direct contradiction to my wishes. Confound you, you won't even use the name you were christened with – your grandfather will be turning in his grave. I've given you every advantage and look how you repay me. I tell you here and now: from this moment on, you are no longer a son of mine."

As he roared out the last words, he saw them cowed before him and gloried in the shock on their blank, stupid faces. Milksops, the lot of them: weak, spineless, worthless.

"Oooh, Freddie darling, I think you've upset him," one of the fawning women cooed.

4

"Then if that's how you feel," Freddie replied defiantly, "that must be the end of it. Goodbye, Father. I shall continue to celebrate with my friends. I wish I could say the last twenty-five years have been a pleasure."

Seething, he raised his swagger stick as if to strike his son, who stared back without flinching. But he thought better of it.

"Then you can go to blazes!" he hurled back. "The lot of you!"

He turned on his heel and stormed off. The bar-hangers moved obediently aside to create a path for him, everyone staring dumbly in his direction. He barged into a woman in the doorway, middle-aged, in the hat and uniform of a district nurse. She was staring at him in open-mouthed alarm, and, quickly realising that she could have no part in this mayhem, he touched the peak of his cap, by way of an apology.

"Good day to you, madam. I advise you to keep well away from this – this den of iniquity."

He charged out on to the pavement, scattering passers-by. He wrenched open the rear door of the waiting staff car, clambered in and slammed it so hard that the whole vehicle rocked. Barking at the driver to pull away and be quick about it, he felt glad that every yard he travelled widened the gulf between him and the thankless wretch who had been his son.

His mind was made up: that gulf would never be bridged.

And he was a man of his word.

Paxham, Devon 1970

1

I'd no idea where I'd been heading: Cornwall, possibly. I'd simply hopped on a train and travelled aimlessly, because that was my outlook these days.

Then I'd happened to see the little fishing village, as the train had rolled into the station. I took in its quiet harbour, a little stone-built chapel tucked into a corner, the narrow streets sloping down to a tiny patch of beach. It didn't strike me as a place of any particular beauty. Paxham. I recalled that 'pax' was the Latin word for 'peace'. And I was looking for peace. I got off the train there.

The small hotel I came upon was called Harbour Heights, and, quite properly, it looked down over the harbour. Nothing grand, but it was quiet and scrupulously clean. I booked in for a few nights, left my bags and strolled down to the chapel in the corner of the harbour.

I think my first view of the chapel from the train was what had drawn me to Paxham. It was unpretentious, and I was struck by its sense of doughty isolation, the grime-dappled stone walls, the worn brown pews, the simple communion table covered with an ancient baize cloth, the rough wooden cross hanging on the wall above it.

Outside, a ferry boat chugged languidly across the wide estuary of the River Lees to the sprawling town of Leesbourne; while in the harbour, the moored fishing boats jigged up and down to the swell of water slopping against the quay. Farther out, the September sun turned the sea to gold.

I sat on the front pew, closed my eyes and sighed. How my life had changed since the diagnosis! But they'd caught the cancer early, the operation had been successful, and the only dark blot was that there could be no guarantee against its return in the years ahead.

I'd been twenty-four years old and consumed with bitterness. For a while, that creeping shadow had engulfed my whole life. The long illness had forced me to give up my job, but perhaps the cruellest blow of all had been that, while I'd lain recovering in hospital, my girlfriend had found someone else.

Mum and Dad had been tremendously supportive, but I'd felt the need to get away for a while, rediscover who I was and gradually return to life. As I'd expected, they hadn't stood in my way, and I'd withdrawn my savings, set out from the little Oxfordshire town of my birth and headed – well, anywhere, in the hope that I'd return with purpose and without bitterness.

Perhaps that was asking a lot.

I started at the heavy click of the latch and the thud of the chapel door closing. Looking round, I saw that someone had come in: a grey-haired woman in blue kagoule and walking boots, a woolly hat on her head. We threw one another a brief smile, as she laid her backpack and walking pole on the floor beside the door. She began to wander around the chapel.

I returned to my reflections, silently offering up my usual prayer, but within moments I looked up at a sharp intake of breath from my fellow visitor. She was standing before a shiny brass plaque on the chapel's side wall. I guessed it commemorated the names of those who'd given their lives in the two World Wars.

The woman glanced across and smiled apologetically. "I'm sorry. I didn't mean to startle you. There was – a name I recognised. Oh, the poor lamb."

I smiled back uncertainly and, as I returned to my solitude, heard the swish of her clothing as she sat down on a pew. Within minutes, she was on her feet again and plodded back to the rear of the chapel. I heard the striking of a match, the deep *plop* of coins descending into the iron chest near the door.

Once she'd gone, I stood and saw she'd lit a candle. Wondering idly who it was for, I moved across to examine the names on the plaque. About twenty were listed, the names of those who'd perished in the Paxham-Leesbourne ferry sinking in May 1949. *Twenty-one years ago.* I wondered whose name she'd recognised.

Leaving the chapel, I wandered around the village. There wasn't a lot to it, the narrow streets twisting up from the harbour, the few shops already closed for the day, apart from the little supermarket. I walked back to Harbour Heights. Dinner was at seven, and I wanted to freshen up and change my shirt beforehand.

I was greeted by the landlady, with whom I'd booked in earlier. Eleanor Neale was fiftyish and looked forbidding, her greying hair worn in a bun. I suspected that her shrewd dark eyes missed very little. Her manner was pleasant, however, and appearances could be deceptive.

"Ah, Mr Verney. I've put you in Number Six. It's two flights up, but I'm sure you won't mind the climb?"

"Not at all."

"Have a good look round the village?"

"Yes, thanks. Quiet and peaceful, which is what I'm looking for."

Eleanor Neale was about to ask a further question, pinning me with an intense gaze, when we were interrupted by the door beyond reception buffeting open. A girl appeared, looking frazzled.

"I've done the spuds, Miss Neale. Ought I to put 'em on now?"

"Well, they won't cook if you don't, Holly," Eleanor replied archly. The girl caught sight of me and smiled shyly. "This is Holly Tasker, Mr Verney," Eleanor went on. "She helps me out around here."

We both said "Hi" simultaneously. I guessed we were about the same age. She was quite pretty, face lightly freckled and her blonde hair parted in the middle and tied in bunches at the sides. Her brown eyes appraised me briefly before looking away.

"I'd better get on," she said.

"Yes, you better had," her employer remarked wryly.

Holly whisked round and disappeared into the kitchen. Her stained and rumpled apron reached mid-calf, but her rear view revealed a short dark skirt and two shapely legs. A polite cough from Miss Neale reclaimed my attention.

"And don't forget the carrots," she called after the girl. "A bit crunchy the other night. And there's eight of us tonight, including you and me."

"Right-o, Miss Neale," came the reply from the depths of the kitchen.

Eleanor shook her head, stifling a smile. "More used to working in pubs, that one. Irene Pake, down at the Lobster Pot, sent her up here when she turned up out of the blue looking for work. Pleasant enough lass, and I can't fault her for effort. Well, Mr Verney, like I said, dinner's at seven, as long as she gets that veg cooked in time." She fixed me with a searching look. "Hope you don't mind me saying so, but you look a bit peaky. Just getting over an illness, perhaps?"

It occurred to me that my hostess was an inveterate gatherer of information. I hoped I was going to like her but was reluctant to talk about my illness. However, under her relentless scrutiny, I felt I ought to say something.

"I've -er, been in hospital for a while. My doctor recommended I take a long holiday to set myself right, so here I am. A bit of walking, bit of sketching – nothing too strenuous."

Eleanor was smiling warmly. "Then the sea air should do you a power of good."

"That's what I'm hoping," I replied and, taking the proffered key, picked up my bags and escaped to my room.

2

At seven o'clock precisely, an apologetic-sounding gong summoned me to the dining room. It was a smallish room, crammed with half-a-dozen tables, each covered with a red-and-white gingham cloth. The wide bay window looked down on to the harbour, although the window table was the preserve of two twittery, middle-aged spinsters: Miss Gibbs, tall and ascetic-looking, and the rotund, perpetually smiling Miss Moriarty. Both greeted me with gracious nods, as did the other two guests, an elderly clergyman and his wife.

I'd just parked myself at a vacant table, when another guest walked in. We recognised one another simultaneously. It was the lady I'd met in the harbour chapel less than an hour earlier. She'd shed her walking gear and looked comfortably smart in thin blue cardigan, crisp white blouse and grey woollen skirt.

"We meet again," she said, as she took a seat at the table next to mine. "Life seems full of coincidences."

Her warm smile set me at ease. "Have you been here long?" I asked, feeling a little awkward.

"Oh, just two days. It's cosy and without airs. Miss Neale and her young helper look after us very well. Are you here on holiday, Mr -?"

"Er, Verney. Aidan Verney. Yes, stopping off for a few days on my way down to Cornwall."

"Miss Instow – Constance. I was in Cornwall back in the spring for a short break. Beautiful coastline, both north and south. But I'm enjoying Devon too." She sighed. "Our country has much to recommend it."

Dinner was, like Harbour Heights itself, palatable and without frills: vegetable soup, then shepherd's pie, followed by jam sponge and ice cream. Eleanor Neale was pleased that Miss Instow and I had struck up a conversation, and Miss Instow explained that we'd met briefly in the harbour chapel that afternoon.

9

Holly served dinner briskly and cheerfully, although the clergyman's wife seemed unimpressed by the brevity of her skirt. Constance Instow had a few words with the girl in passing, again in a kindly way, trying to draw her out a little, but Holly was too busy dashing to and from the kitchen to make conversation.

Turning to me, Miss Instow asked if I was taking a holiday for health reasons.

"Why, does it show?" I replied nervously. But I knew that it did, knew it'd be a while before I'd be back to anything like I'd been before my illness. *If at all.*

She smiled wryly. "I don't mean to intrude. I was a district nurse for many years, you see, and have a nose for these things."

I gabbled a hasty disclaimer. "Please – you're not intruding at all. Yes, I'm recovering from an illness."

The other guests were deep in their own conversations, and I confided some details of my illness to Miss Instow. She listened sympathetically, and I found myself warming to her. It felt good to open up about it. I'd avoided previous opportunities to discuss it, perhaps in the naïve hope that, in keeping quiet, it might completely go away.

We were soon on first-name terms, and she insisted on my calling her Connie. "Constance is a bit of a mouthful." This felt unusual as, back home, I'd always been brought up to address older adults formally, which was certainly the case in the store where I'd worked. But that was the thing about Connie Instow: she seemed interested in people for who they were.

Perhaps I hadn't intended to divulge so much but I felt that, with her, any information was in safe hands. I tried to sound upbeat: I'd got off the train at Paxham on a whim and was looking forward to doing a fair bit of walking and sketching. Beyond that, I had no further plans. I deliberately left out any mention of Diana, her defection, my emptiness and regrets. Those matters had no place in the little dining room this evening.

Connie was a good listener. She wished me well and promised to hold me in her prayers.

She talked a little of herself. She'd lived in London all her life, had retired five years previously and was now helping in a Seamen's Mission in Rotherhithe. A brother who lived nearby was her only surviving relative.

"I'd been cooped up in London for years and promised myself that in retirement I'd get out and see the country. Old habits die hard, but I've managed a number of expeditions." She named Offa's Dyke, the Pennine Way and the Dorset coast path among these, and I remarked that she hadn't done badly. Connie had explored a few local routes since arriving in Paxham and promised to pass some details on to me.

Miss Neale announced that she'd serve coffee in the lounge, once dinner was over. The clergyman and his wife waived the invitation, but Misses Gibbs and Moriarty sped ahead to nab the window seat, with the excuse that they needed the last of the light for their knitting.

I'd taken Connie Instow into my confidence and was pleasantly surprised when, as we settled in armchairs suitably distanced from the rhythmic click of needles, she returned the compliment.

"When we were in the chapel earlier," she said, "I recognised a name on the memorial plaque." She leaned towards me, close enough for me to see tears in her eyes. "I'm sure it's the same boy," she went on. "He and his mother lived in Deptford during the war, the father missing presumed dead, on active service. They were among my patients. Georgie Kell was a lovely little boy, and his mother sadly very ill. She needed a change of air for her health's sake but insisted on staying put in the hope that her husband would return safely at the end of the war.

"Unfortunately, he didn't. His body was recovered, identified, and his widow had to accept it. I was quite close to her and persuaded her to move to her sister's in Paxham. She'd been widowed too and was more than happy to take them in. They moved the year after the war ended, when Georgie would have been about three, but his mother's condition deteriorated, and she died during the bitter winter of 1947. Georgie was looked after by his aunt, but it appears that he was a victim of that terrible ferry tragedy."

Just at that moment, Holly came over with our coffees. She flicked me a nervous smile, then turned to Connie. "Miss Instow, I'm sorry, but I couldn't help overhearing what you were saying about the ferry sinking. Mrs Bayldon at the Manor lost her daughter that day, although her grandson, Edward, was rescued. It was a terrible tragedy, and people in the village still talk about it."

"That's all right, dear," Connie replied gently. "I met Ruth Bayldon while out walking today, and she invited me to the Manor for a cup of tea tomorrow afternoon."

"Then I expect you'll be off for another ramble in the morning?" Holly seemed eager to change the subject. She'd been hovering quite near us, and I wondered if she'd spoken initially in case we suspected her of deliberately eavesdropping.

The thought didn't appear to have crossed Connie's mind. "Oh, I shall be on my way straight after breakfast," she declared breezily. "I've been told there are some pretty hamlets along the Lees estuary. And that I'll be able to get back to Paxham across the fields. Which reminds me, Aidan: I'll leave those leaflets I promised you with Miss Neale at reception."

Holly turned towards me, smiling shyly. "Are you a rambler too, Mr Verney."

I returned the smile with equal uncertainty. My illness had drained me of confidence, and that and the loss of Diana had made me feel awkward in the company of people of my own age. "Er, yes, I hope to do some walking. Er, some sketching too."

Her eyes widened. "Then you're an *artist?*"

I laughed. It sounded strange, because I hadn't done that in a while. But the awe in her tone strangely lifted me. "Nothing so grand," I went on. "It's no more than doodling, really. I've – well, been ill for a while, and I'm finding it good therapy."

"Then you might try the harbour – the fishing boats and everything, and there's a smashing view across the estuary."

"Thanks. I will." I tried to hold her gaze, but she quickly looked away at a comment from Connie.

"Are you from London, too, Holly?"

She giggled self-consciously. "My accent must stand out a mile. East London, born and bred."

"It's my home, too – south of the river. There's so much to see outside it, and I'm only finding that out in retirement."

"I was looking for a change as well. I've been here four months, and Nelly – oops, sorry! – Miss Neale has been really kind. Anyway, I must get on with clearing away."

Holly disappeared back into the dining room, and Connie suggested a few more places for sketching.

"And if you're looking for refreshment, try the Lobster Pot down beyond the quay," she said. "It's a pleasant location, particularly on a warm day. I was so thirsty yesterday afternoon that I stopped off for a glass of lemonade. I'm a teetotaller, so normally wouldn't have set foot in there."

Her face suddenly clouded in a frown, and for a moment it seemed that she'd forgotten I was there. I shifted in my chair, preparing to get up. "I think I'll go out for a breath of air before bed," I said.

"Yes." Connie was back with me, smiling. "I think I've walked enough for one day. An early night's called for. Thanks for your company, Aidan. And take my advice. Don't stay in one place too long. I did, and I regret that, in a way. There's so much to marvel at and enjoy."

I guessed she was referring to her years in London, a city whose frenetic pace had never greatly appealed to me. I remarked that it was a big place and that it could be quite stifling.

"Indeed," Connie answered. "But it's a small world."

We said our goodnights then, and I wandered through the narrow streets, where only the pubs seemed anything like busy. Tiredness soon began to kick in, and before long I made my way back to Harbour Heights. As I walked along the road above the quay, I happened to look across and see a familiar figure sitting on a bench beside the chapel.

It was Holly. Half-heartedly, I raised a hand in greeting, but she didn't notice me. She was gazing out across the harbour, and I felt there was something forlorn about her glum expression.

I hesitated, wondering if I might go down and have a word with her. But, in my inimitable way, I thought better of it, turned away and returned to the hotel.

3

By the time I got down to breakfast, Connie Instow had already departed. As promised, she'd left some details outlining walks around Paxham.

"Oh, you missed her by a good half-hour," Eleanor Neale informed me, as she served up bacon, egg, sausage and fried bread. "All kitted out for a day striding over the cliffs. Got a sight more energy than I have, and that's a fact."

I gratefully accepted her offer of a packed lunch, as I expected to be out for much of the day. Holly handed it over as I made my way out a little later, sketchpad tucked under my arm.

"Be sure to show me what you draw." I'd not seen her at breakfast but had heard sounds of her industry in the kitchen. She seemed chirpier this morning, not quite so withdrawn. I returned her smile. Going by some of my earlier efforts, I doubted she'd be impressed.

I walked for over an hour, returning to a grassy bank above the harbour. Away to the right, a steep, winding path, punctuated with wooden benches for the out-of-breath, struggled up to the tops of the red sandstone cliffs, which stretched out along the bay. Below, an assortment of fishing boats were moored beside the quay, seagulls wheeling and screeching above it, and the foot passenger ferry chugged its unhurried way across the estuary to the town of Leesbourne.

A narrow lane led up from the far end of the quay, passing a clutch of cottages before disappearing into woodland. From the map in Connie's leaflet, it looked as if it ran parallel to the estuary, before turning inland at the next village, circling behind Paxham to lead back to the cliffs a couple of miles beyond.

There was a pub just beyond the quay too, which Miss Neale and Connie Instow had mentioned: The Lobster Pot, a squat, cosy-looking building, thatched and newly whitewashed, with a sprawl of wooden tables and benches outside, its surroundings appropriately littered with the drying nets and lobster pots of the local fishermen.

Connie had recommended dropping in there, so I polished off my sandwiches and set off down to the pub to slake my thirst.

It had just turned midday, and the pub was quiet. A group of fishermen in woolly hats and shirtsleeves were engaged in a game of darts beyond the bar, whose sole occupant was leaning comfortably on it, a pewter tankard at his elbow, as he conversed with the woman behind the bar.

She saw me come in, abruptly curtailed the conversation and made her way towards me. I placed her in her forties, dark-haired with high cheekbones and black eyes, which glinted with a challenge. I suspected that her firmly set mouth didn't readily expand into a smile.

Still, her manner was civil enough, and she served me briskly with a shandy, going so far as to make a stab at conversation. "You're new to the Lobster. Down here on holiday?" There was a combative edge to her voice, making me wary of supplying any answer other than what she expected.

"Yes, I'm staying at Harbour Heights."

She gave a curt nod at the sketchpad which I'd rested on the bar. "An artist too, I see. We get our fair share."

"In a very amateur way. But it's an enjoyable hobby."

"Harbour Heights is my sister's place." The bar-hanger had edged his way towards me, wearing a wide grin. He was huge, a good head taller than me, and looked every inch a fisherman with a sunburnt, weathered face and an unruly mop of what must have been blond hair but had, in middle age, turned practically white.

He held out a hand, which I shook, his grip uncompromising. "Jim Neale, though on account o' this thatch, folks call me Snowy. Hope our Nell's treating you all right?"

"Aidan Verney. Yes, thanks. I'm very comfortable there."

"You'll have met young Holly, then," Snowy grinned. "Tidy little lass. Come looking for bar work, and Irene here sent her up to our Nell. Glad it's working out."

"Drew the line at employing another blinkin' Londoner," Irene said sullenly. "One's almost too many. Besides, what's London ever done for me?" She glanced at the clock above the door. "Speaking of which -?"

At that moment, the beaded curtain behind the bar swished back, and a woman bustled through, slightly out of breath.

"Phew! Sorry I'm late, Irene."

15

"I was about to give up on you, Bet," Irene grumbled. "At least we're not busy yet and, thanks to me, the sandwiches got done early." She glared at the newcomer. "Just in case you were late. Again."

The woman called Bet threw me a smile. She was probably Irene's age but must once have been very pretty, with a rich tumble of auburn hair. Her lacy white blouse was low-cut enough to arouse the immediate interest of Snowy and the darts players. Irene seemed less impressed, scowling at the big fisherman.

"You down on holiday, lovey?" Bet asked me, unfazed by both kinds of attention she was receiving.

"He's already told us he is," Irene cut in irritably. "If you'd got here on time you'd have heard. His name's Aidan, before you ask. And now look after the bar, while I fetch the food through. I doubt if Snowy'll object."

Bet raised her eyebrows, and Snowy looked amused, as Irene stomped away, barging through the curtain into the far reaches of the pub.

"Nice to meet you, Aidan." Bet kept her voice low. "Might not see me here again. Reckon I'm for the high jump."

"Ah, you're too valuable, our Bet, and she knows it," Snowy weighed in gallantly. "That's Irene Pake's way and has been for all the years I've known her. Her bark's much worse than her bite."

"And that's pretty fierce." Bet's smile was still trained on me. "Bet Parrish, lovey. Hope you enjoy Paxham. We're a friendly bunch – well, excepting Irene. Still, she's not a bad sort to work for, and I've known far worse."

"Aidan Verney," I said. "So, you and Holly are both Londoners."

"S'pose the accent's a dead giveaway," Bet laughed. "Yep. Didn't know Holly before she turned up here, but we'd both got fed up with life in the smoke. I'm glad she got fixed up with Nell. I was afraid for a minute that Irene would take her on and give me the push."

"As I just said, you're too valuable." Snowy's face wore a cheeky grin. "Dunno what we'd do here without you. Probably give up and do our drinking in the Boatman."

She gave his straying hand a playful slap. "Probably wouldn't let you take such liberties there, Snowy Neale. Get away with you. Pity you're not chapel like your sainted sister. In here propping up the bar every spare minute."

More people were drifting in, as Irene returned with a tray of pork pies, pasties and thick-cut sandwiches. Suddenly, she and Bet were busy. I finished my shandy and turned to go. Bet broke off what she was doing to offer a cheery wave, while Snowy called out to me to pop back in before long.

I went back to my original spot on the bank and made a sketch of the pub and quayside. I think I must have taken more care over it than usual, because I felt I could allow other eyes to see it. Holly, I was sure, was bound to ask.

4

As I worked away at my drawing, my attention was drawn to a man strolling along the quay. He looked very tanned, slick dark hair curling down over his collar, and walked with a swagger, a denim jacket slung carelessly over one shoulder. He kept switching glances about him, as if sizing up the surroundings. I watched as he wandered into the Lobster Pot, to emerge minutes later with a foaming pint glass. Depositing his jacket on a bench, he sat and sampled his beer, nodding affably at a couple seated nearby.

When Bet came out to clear away empty glasses, the man looked up and spoke to her. It was a brief exchange, but Bet didn't give him the time of day, whisking up her tray and flouncing back into the pub to his obvious amusement. He soon drank up and sauntered back towards the village.

I finished off my sketch and decided to take a short walk before heading back to Harbour Heights for a nap. My doctor had prescribed plenty of rest and, while I felt tired, I also felt invigorated by the sea air and the morning's activities.

*

I found Connie Instow in a sombre mood at dinner that evening. She'd enjoyed her ramble, stopping to eat her lunch in one of the hamlets on the banks of the Lees, before skirting round behind Paxham to meet the cliff path at the medieval chapel of St Audric's, now a ruin, from where she'd walked down to meet Mrs Bayldon at Paxham Manor.

She'd spoken to her hostess about Georgie Kell, the little boy who'd died in the ferry tragedy, and while Mrs Bayldon had appeared stoical, Connie had been saddened by her story.

"I wish I hadn't mentioned Georgie. The poor woman tried hard not to show it, but the memories of that awful day will never leave her."

The Bayldons had long been the village's leading lights, the Manor having been in Roderick Bayldon's family for two hundred years. Their son-in-law, a captain in the British Army, had been killed in the D-Day landings, and their daughter Madeleine had moved back to the Manor with her small son, Edward. Madeleine had died in the ferry sinking, although Edward had been rescued, to be brought up by his grandparents.

"Apparently, Madeleine lost her life in an attempt to save another little boy," Connie went on. "Mrs Bayldon didn't say, but I'm sure that must have been Georgie."

"It's all so very sad. Colonel Bayldon was utterly devoted to his daughter, and never properly recovered from the loss. The poor man passed away two years ago. Still, the tragedy spurred him into helping those who'd been bereaved, so maybe some good came of it. And, of course, they had Edward and were grateful for that. He was away yesterday, visiting his paternal grandfather, who's in a nursing home in Eastbourne. It's a pity, because I really wanted to meet Edward. I think he's back tomorrow, so perhaps I can arrange to see him then."

Holly was busy serving and clearing away. She'd admired my drawing, but we'd not had much time to chat, as she'd been in the throes of helping prepare dinner. Connie lowered her voice, as the girl bustled past us on her way to the kitchen.

"Holly seems to have taken an interest in Edward, although I get the feeling that she's wasting her time. His grandmother certainly doesn't approve." She smiled bleakly. "Mrs Bayldon believes that she and Edward are a cut above the rest of us, although I believe Holly's a nice enough girl."

I caught the note of doubt in her voice and looked my question.

Connie sighed. "Oh, I don't know, Aidan. Why should a pretty, vivacious girl like her want to come *here*? But I'm being unfair. Why shouldn't she? Perhaps she felt the time was right for a change of scene."

I nodded vacantly, for my thoughts were on another track. I knew Mrs Bayldon's type only too well. Of course, Holly, with her East London roots, wouldn't be deemed good enough for her precious grandson. I'd been down that road myself. *"What are your prospects, young man?"* Diana's banker father had asked. He'd seemed unimpressed when I'd replied that I hoped to be promoted to departmental supervisor in the store where I'd worked since school. Obviously, Diana's fiancé – yes, she'd lost no time in picking up with someone else and getting engaged, talk about indecent haste! – slotted into the right category: he'd just qualified as an accountant.

Connie was still speaking, and I felt duty bound to listen. Alone, I'd have lapsed into a black mood, made the escape to my room, so that I could feel sorry for myself there. Life was just so unfair. *Why me? Why me?* That self-inflicted, doom-sodden mantra echoed in my head. I tried to pull myself together. None of this was Connie's fault, after all.

"General Hambling's very old, ill and extremely rich. Edward stands to inherit everything before long. Mrs Bayldon is sure he'll restore Paxham Manor to its former glory. From what I saw, it seems to be falling down around their ears."

I caught the note of regret in her voice, but she didn't take the matter any further. By then, we'd finished dinner, and Connie had decided not to venture out that evening, as a strong wind was blowing in off the sea. She suggested coffee in the lounge and, with a sly peek at Gibbs and Moriarty, who were still on their dessert, wondered if we might be so bold as to nab the window seat? The clergyman and his wife had moved on to pastures new earlier that day, so there was no-one else who might stand in our way.

Once in the lounge, Connie made sure of the window seat, while I went to collect our coffees. A man sat on a stool, leaning masterfully on the bar; while Holly, on the other side of it, was looking hunted.

On sensing my approach, the man turned, and I immediately recognised him as the customer I'd seen sitting outside the Lobster Pot that afternoon.

Holly threw me a distracted smile. "I'll bring your coffees over in a minute."

"Oh, there's no hurry."

I was aware of the newcomer appraising me and turned to face him.

"Hi there, young man." His manner was exuberant, and I had no way or reason to ignore his outstretched hand, which I shook dutifully. "Tony's the name. Tony Delverton."

Another Londoner. It made me wonder if London was being evacuated again. "Aidan Verney. Are you a guest here too?"

"Oh, I dare say." I found myself immediately disliking his cocksure attitude. He jerked a thumb at the scowling Holly. "Y'know, I looked at this pretty miss and reckoned she'd pull a good pint. All she offers me is a bottle of light ale."

"That's because it's all we have," came the starchy response. "If you want draught beer, you'll find it at the Lobster Pot just past the quay."

"Oh, I already have, darling. And I mean to try the Boatman in the High Street, too." He chuckled lewdly. "Nice scenery at the Lobster. Almost as nice as here. Ah, well, s'pose I'd better love you and leave you. You make sure you're a good girl, now."

He turned, winked at me and grinned, as he slipped down off the stool. Then his expression changed. For a moment, I registered something like alarm on his smug features, but he quickly resumed his swagger. "Better get along there, 'fore I die of thirst." He strode off into reception, slamming the outer door behind him.

Holly looked harassed but managed a quick smile. "I'll fetch your coffees over. Oh, here come the ladies. I'll do theirs too." She turned towards the coffee maker behind the bar.

I went back to Connie, who was staring in the direction Tony Delverton had gone. She didn't seem aware of my approach, and I distinctly caught her whispered words: "*Surely* – not the two of them?"

In her distraction, she hadn't noticed that her handbag had fallen off the seat. I stooped to retrieve it, and as she noticed the movement, she came to life. "Oh, how careless of me. Thank you, Aidan."

I handed her the contents: a purse, mirror, lace handkerchief, peppermints and a badly creased black-and-white photograph, all which she restored to her handbag, fastening the clasp.

I took my seat, remarking that Paxham seemed to have its fair share of Londoners. I was fishing for a comment about Delverton, whom I felt sure she must have recognised from somewhere.

But Connie couldn't be drawn. She exchanged pleasantries with the ladies and went on to talk about the walk she intended to do the next day. Holly brought the coffees over and started to make her way back to the kitchen, as Eleanor Neale walked in.

<h1 style="text-align:center">5</h1>

Holly stopped her in the doorway, looking anxious. I hadn't intended to eavesdrop, but Connie and I were sitting so close by that we couldn't help overhearing.

"Oh, Miss Neale. The man who just left, the one who was at the bar. He's not staying here, is he?"

"Mr Delverton? Yes, he booked in earlier, when you were preparing dinner. Down here on business, apparently. Why, what's the matter?"

I saw dismay on Holly's face. She made a poor show of shrugging it off. "Oh, it's nothing. I'll start clearing away now, shall I?"

"Yes, please, dear."

Eleanor Neale watched her go and turned towards us. "What was all that about?"

I was wondering the same. "I don't think she appreciated Mr Delverton's manner," I replied diplomatically.

Eleanor sniffed. "Well, like so many girls, she *will* wear these short skirts. Recipe for trouble, if you ask me. Nobody'd catch me wearing one!" She was oblivious to the tight smiles which Connie and I exchanged. "I do hope Mr Delverton's not going to be troublesome," she went on. "Asked if we had telephones in the bedrooms, if ever you did! I told him straight – use the pay phone in reception, like everybody else."

Once she'd gone, Connie and I drank our coffees and resumed our conversation. I wondered if she'd allude to Delverton. She didn't mention him, but her manner seemed a little distant, as if she had something on her mind. Before long, we called it a night.

I slept well and was up in good time for breakfast, thinking to make an early start and rest up for a while in the afternoon, as I'd done the previous day. Connie Instow was in reception, as I came out of the dining room. She was off on a long ramble, taking the cliff path up past the Manor and beyond St Audric's chapel to Ackland Point, from which, on a clear day, views far down the Devon coastline were possible.

Tony Delverton came past as we were talking. He nodded a greeting and paused to pick up a newspaper off the reception desk. The blaring headline suggested news of a further clash between the IRA and British troops in Belfast. He pitched it back carelessly on to the desk and plodded into the dining room. I guessed he hadn't sampled just the one pint in the Lobster Pot the previous evening.

With a cheerful farewell, Connie set off, and Holly emerged from the kitchen to greet me with a smile, then groan as she caught sight of Delverton hunched over one of the tables and squinting at the menu.

"Oh, Miss Neale?" the girl called back through the swinging door. "Would you mind serving Mr Delverton, please?"

"Leave him to me, dear." Eleanor came bustling out. "He'll get the shock of his life if he tries pinching *my* posterior."

"Thanks, Miss Neale." Holly turned to me, dredging up a smile. "Where are you heading this morning?" she asked.

"Miss Instow suggested a walk along the estuary. She says a couple of hamlets on the banks are worth seeing."

"Oh, yes. Hobbs Reach is really pretty – well, I like it. And it's not too far away. I should imagine you'll be sketching?"

"I dare say."

"Then I'll want to see what you draw. You're really very good, you know?"

I thanked her, doubting that I deserved the compliment. But I was grateful, because it lifted me a little.

"I -er, I hope everything's okay," I bumbled, directing a nod towards the dining room.

Her smile seemed forced. "Oh – *him?* Just the type, I'm afraid – taking liberties. I just wasn't in the mood to put up with it. But thanks for asking." She seemed to brighten a little. "Would you like me to make you some sarnies?"

"Yes – yes, thanks, I would."

22

"I'll have them ready when you come back down."

I thanked her again and went upstairs to collect my things, smiling to myself. I was no artist, and Holly was being kind, but in the past weeks, sketching had become a pastime in which I could lose myself and my cares for a while and put the future on hold. It was a bolt hole, where I could feel at peace.

The walk along the estuary gave me a good view of the busy market town of Leesbourne. I felt no inclination to go there, but Connie and Holly had been right about the hamlets. Hobbs Reach and Dulverbank were little clusters of pretty thatched cottages along the river, many with their private jetties and both exuding that unhurried sense of peace, which I was coming to appreciate.

I halted at a bend in the river and tried to capture the sunlight dancing on the water, and the bright skiffs and launches moored along the banks. I put extra effort into my drawing, because Holly wouldn't let me escape showing her my efforts.

I returned to Paxham and called in at the Lobster Pot, just as the lunchtime trade was winding down. I was met with a friendly greeting from both Bet and Snowy, and even Irene Pake was congenial, asking where I'd been that morning. I told them about my walk along the estuary. I'd only covered two or three miles, but it had been enough for me.

"Ah, that nice elderly lady who's staying up at our Nell's is the one," Snowy remarked. "My goodness, hasn't she covered some miles? Nell says she wishes she had half her energy."

"Won't find her leaning on no bar," Bet put in mischievously.

"Or chatting up the customers," Irene observed with something like a wry smile.

"Well, she was off early again this morning," I put in. "Heading over the cliffs to Ackland Point. She should have some fine views on a day like this." I added that I didn't expect the latest guest at Harbour Heights to be quite so energetic, although he did recommend the Lobster Pot.

Snowy's eyes twinkled, as he winked at Bet. "Now, I wonder who he can mean?"

Bet turned away with a dismissive, "Huh! Him!" and went to serve another customer.

Snowy nodded in the direction of Irene, who was busy at the far end of the bar. "Didn't endear himself to Irene either," he said. "And as you'll have worked out, your chum's definitely too forward for Bet's liking."

I grinned back. In his short time in Paxham, Delverton hadn't acquired the knack of winning admirers. And as for him being a chum...

I finished my drink, said my goodbyes and set off. Tiredness was kicking in, because I'd walked farther than I'd intended. As I toiled up from the quay towards Harbour Heights, I noticed a young couple coming down Market Street towards the hotel.

It was with something of a shock that I recognised Holly, pretty in a white minidress with a cardigan around her shoulders. Her companion was about my age. The two of them were walking a yard apart, he striding along with a battered suitcase in one hand, and she scurrying to keep up with him.

My immediate impression was that they didn't belong together, and I presumed the young man was Edward Hambling, heir to the crumbling Paxham Manor.

Holly noticed me and waved, hurrying to intercept me at the street corner. Edward followed with obvious reluctance. I guessed my somewhat rumpled appearance didn't appeal to him.

I recalled a newspaper headline from the turn of the year. It predicted that 1970 would be 'the Year of the Young' and featured a photograph of a long-haired, trendily dressed young couple, posed as if peering into a promising future. In my flares, T-shirt and training shoes, I paid token homage to the departed 1960s; but Edward, with his short back-and-sides, collar, tie and hounds' tooth jacket, seemed firmly entrenched in the 1950s.

"Hi!" Holly greeted me. "This is Edward – I think Miss Instow mentioned him? He lives at the Manor with his gran. Edward Hambling – Aidan Verney. Aidan's a guest at Miss Neale's."

Edward set down his suitcase and offered a formal hand. I was struck by his long, pale fingers and the softness of his grip. "Mr Verney."

"Please to meet you," I replied.

"I've been to meet him from the station," Holly explained. "He's just back from visiting his grandad in Eastbourne."

I was puzzled for a moment, then realised that Holly wasn't referring to the late Colonel Bayldon, but his paternal grandfather, who was in a nursing home. I recalled her previously mentioning him as being very ill.

"Yes, I fear the general's in decline," Edward informed me, his public school voice hardly endearing him to me. Its superior twang made me suspect that he was talking down to me. "Bit of a waste of my time," he added. "But then, I am his only surviving relative, so it is my duty." Edward made it sound as if he'd done his grandfather an enormous favour by going to see him.

An awkward pause ensued, with he and I grinning at one another inanely and without much warmth. Holly rescued the situation.

"Well, I'd better be getting back. Lots to do. Would you like to come in for a cup of tea, Edward?"

"Er, no, thanks. I ought to cut along. Gran's expecting me."

"Fine. See you tomorrow, perhaps?"

"Er, yes, I expect so. Goodbye. Nice meeting you, Mr Verney."

With that, he picked up his suitcase and hurried off down the next street, heading for Paxham Manor.

Holly watched him go. She was frowning distractedly, but the smile was back as she turned to face me. I'd been frowning too, wondering why she should be at all interested in Edward? The reason was beyond me, because, for his part, he seemed to take no interest in her at all.

"Done lots of sketching?" she asked perkily.

"Yes, I'm reasonably pleased with –"

But she'd already slid the pad out from under my arm and was flicking through the pages. "I'm impressed," she declared at last. "I like the one of the boats on the estuary. Are you on your way back to the hotel?"

"Yes. I could do with a bit of a rest, quite honestly."

"Then why don't I make you that cup of tea Edward didn't want?"

"Sounds good."

We walked the short distance to Harbour Heights and hesitated in the doorway. Eleanor Neale was craning over the reception desk, wearing a look of profound concentration. On seeing us, she jabbed an urgent finger towards the lounge.

"Mr - Delverton's -got – a - visitor," she mouthed, as if attempting to explain something to a person who spoke little English.

I could hear the buzz of voices, Delverton's kept deliberately low. As Holly and I stepped discreetly past the lounge's open door, I glimpsed a table strewn with tea things, and Delverton leaning across towards a woman, who appeared distinctly unmoved.

"Oh, come on, Val." Desperation leaked from Delverton's voice, its cockiness a distant memory. "Please, be reasonable. You got to cut me some slack here."

As Holly and I gathered round Eleanor, we heard the shriek of castors, as a chair was pushed back.

"I want it back, Tony." The woman's voice was clear and dispassionate. "I'm having difficulty making ends meet."

"But, sweetheart -?" He was pleading now, an insistent whine. "I'm not asking much. I'm closing in on an important deal. When it's done, I'll let you have it back with interest."

She refused to budge. "How many times have I heard that? One week, Tony, and you pay back what you owe me. After that, I'm having nothing more to do with your schemes, and that's final."

"Oh, but Val -?"

"Enough. I'm going. I've got a train to catch."

She strode out of the lounge, looking unamused, an attractive woman of middle age, the march of time slightly softened by bright lipstick, rouge and dyed black hair. Her jacket and skirt were smart but dowdy.

She flashed a brief smile at the three of us clustered round the desk. "Thanks for the tea." She hurried off in the direction of the station.

26

"You're welcome, ma'am," Eleanor called after her. She threw Holly and me a wicked grin. "It'll be going on his bill, never fear."

Delverton ambled out of the lounge, the cue for Holly to disappear into the kitchen to make the promised tea. I felt it typical that Delverton had left the crockery where it was, for someone else to clear away. He was drawing on a cigarette in an attempt to appear nonchalant.

"My sister," he drawled unconvincingly, nodding towards the street. "Lends me a bit of dosh, then asks for it back two days later." Taking advantage of Eleanor pretending to study her register, he raised his eyebrows at me, mouthed, "*Women!*" and made off in the opposite direction to that which his visitor had taken.

6

Feeling refreshed after a nap, I wrote and addressed the few postcards I'd purchased earlier, then went back downstairs, pre-empting the dinner gong. Eleanor Neale and Holly were standing in reception, looking anxious, and I asked if something was wrong?

"It's Miss Instow," Eleanor replied. "She's not back yet, and before now, she's always returned in good time to freshen up and change for dinner."

I sensed the unspoken request from the wheedling lilt of my hostess's voice. "Would you like me to go and look for her? She gave me a rough idea of her route."

Eleanor's features relaxed a little. "Oh, would you, Mr Verney? It'd be so kind."

"Is it all right if I go along too?" Holly piped up.

"Yes, dear. An extra pair of eyes might be useful. I can sort out the ladies, and Mr Delverton's not back yet. I'll keep your dinners warm."

It had been a dull afternoon, and the light was already fading. A keen breeze swept through the hotel's open doorway. Eleanor fished in a cupboard and handed us torches and kagoules. "You might need both." Holly and I thanked her and hurried out on to the street, where we almost collided with Delverton.

"Hey, steady on!" he exclaimed. "Where's the fire?"

I explained briefly, conscious of Holly hanging back warily. To Delverton's credit, he offered to come with us, and we waited while he went in to borrow a torch. He

27

re-joined us, panting slightly as we marched up the hill leading out of the village. His breath testified that he'd sunk a swift pint or two before returning for dinner. "Any idea where she might have got to?" he asked.

I recalled that Connie's intention had been to take the cliff path above the Manor and head for St Audric's chapel, continuing along to Ackland Point. It was a distance of six or seven miles, and I felt sure she'd come back the same way, which meant her return to Harbour Heights was long overdue.

"Maybe she's tripped and sprained her ankle?" Holly suggested, the first words she'd spoken since Delverton had joined us.

"Let's hope it's nothing worse than that," I replied grimly. I paused, gazing up at the sandstone cliffs towering above us. "It's a bit of a climb," I went on. "But Miss Instow said the path widens once we reach the top."

To our right a short distance away, stood Paxham Manor. It looked ghostly in the fading light, a stark, grey building with tall, ancient chimneys. As we threaded our path through the wooded area skirting the grounds, Holly spoke again. "Why don't I fetch Edward? He knows the area better than any of us."

I told her to go ahead. Darkness wasn't far off, and once we reached the higher ground, there was a chance that Connie might have strayed off the path. I guessed, too, that Holly distrusted Delverton's presence and felt there'd be safety in numbers.

As the girl departed, Delverton drew alongside me and watched her go. "Hhmm, tasty. What d'you reckon, then, Aidan? Should imagine a young blade like you'd be mighty interested in that?"

"She's a nice girl," I replied blandly. "I like her."

He threw me a greasy smile. "Yeah. I bet you do."

I turned and moved a little way along the path, signalling that the conversation was over.

The Manor's front door was about a hundred yards distant, the driveway below us sweeping round between huge iron gates, which I suspected were no longer capable of closing. Even in the dimness, the grounds looked unkempt, reminiscent of the set for a haunted house movie. It surprised me that Delverton, the entrepreneur, hadn't scented an opportunity along those lines. Although, of course, he might already have done so.

From where we stood, we heard the anguished protest of the front door opening. From behind it, the gangling frame of Edward Hambling appeared. The urgency of Holly's plea was clear, even though her words were whipped away on the breeze. Edward nodded and ducked back inside to re-emerge with a windcheater folded over his arm.

There was no difficulty hearing the strident voice which demanded to know where he was going.

A second figure appeared at the door, an austere-looking woman, whom I took to be Ruth Bayldon. Holly seemed to be explaining the situation rapidly, and the woman nodded her gracious assent. The moment Edward had stepped outside, the door closed firmly.

Within a couple of minutes, he'd joined us, Holly tagging along behind him. He greeted me with a brusque nod and, once Holly had cautiously introduced them, couldn't ignore Delverton's outstretched hand. His gaze seemed to linger on Edward in a predatory way.

"Nice to meet you, Eddie. The name's Tony."

"I prefer to be called Edward," he declared rather pompously.

Delverton grinned tightly and swept on. "Best crack on now we've all met."

As we came out of the patch of woodland to join the path leading up to the cliffs, I let Holly and Edward walk in front. I didn't think I was going to like Edward, but it was useful to have him in our search party.

Once at the top, with Delverton deservedly wheezing a little way behind, the ribbon of path unwound before us, disappearing into hollows and reappearing again. Open fields fell away to our right towards the road from Paxham, from which we heard the sound of occasional traffic.

The path rose steeply through scrub, while below to our left, the sea shimmered bewitchingly, stretching away into a gathering darkness, which was relieved infrequently by the lights of a passing ship.

We began to use our torches, Holly and Edward scanning the fields to the right, while I kept to the path, a few yards from the edge, aware of Delverton panting beerily along in my wake.

The path narrowed, leading us down to a tiny inlet, which we crossed by way of stepping-stones. We searched around for a few minutes but found no sign of Connie. As we struggled back to the top, I caught sight of the silhouette of a small building some way ahead.

Edward had seen me looking. "St Audric's chapel," he said. "She may have stopped there for a rest."

They'd been my thoughts exactly. By now, my concern for Connie's well-being had grown enormously. We agreed to carry out a careful search around the chapel ruins. If she'd got into difficulties, it would be the most likely place she'd have stopped to rest. The alternative had been nipping at my thoughts since we'd set out: that Connie had slipped and plunged over the edge of the cliffs.

We searched diligently, the crazy dance of our torch beams seeming to add a note of despair to our efforts.

"Is there any kind of shelter at Ackland Point?" I asked, recalling that it had been Connie's intention to make for there.

Edward shook his head. "It's open to the elements," he replied. The four of us exchanged glances: we were all beginning to believe the worst.

Because of this, we slowed our pace to a crawl, following the same formation as previously. Delverton and I walked as close to the edge as we dared, noting that the path had eroded badly in places.

Suddenly, my torch beam lit upon a flash of white below the clifftop. My first thought was that it was a piece of litter, but as I stooped, crouched and leaned over the edge, I picked her out. She was lying on a broad ledge some ten feet down.

I called out, my voice feeble and shrill in the gathering gloom, but strong enough to alert everyone.

Delverton came puffing up, followed by the others. "Find her?" he asked.

"She's down there," I replied. "And not moving. She might have slipped on this loose gravel. The path's badly worn just here." I looked around at their pale faces. "We should call an ambulance."

To my surprise, Edward was decisive. "I'll dash back and phone from the Manor. The track from the chapel leads up to the road. Someone ought to go there to direct the ambulance."

"I'll do it," Holly volunteered. She shot me a glance. "Are you all right to wait here?"

"I'm going to try to get down to her." I looked at Delverton. "Can you lower me down some of the way? There seem to be decent footholds."

"For goodness' sake, be careful," Holly warned.

I felt touched by her concern. "I will. Edward, you ought to get moving."

He nodded and left. Holly remained, looking at me anxiously.

"It's okay," I reassured her. "It's probably seven or eight feet down. I'm pretty light, and the ledge is wide. I'll take it slowly. All right, Mr Delverton?"

Holly smiled nervously and started towards the chapel. I waited until the darkness had swallowed her, then knelt at the cliff edge and peered over.

Delverton, breathing heavily, crouched beside me. "Surely, she's too far down for us to get her up?" he observed.

"I wouldn't even try," I replied. "But I feel someone should go down and wait with her."

"You reckon she's alive, then?"

"I hope so. It's not a long drop to the ledge. Can you start to lower me down? I'll try to find a foothold."

"Sure. Hang on a mo'." Delverton peeled off his jacket and laid it on the turf, while I rolled over on to my stomach and began to wriggle down over the loose gravel. Delverton seized my arm in a meaty grasp. I found one foothold, then a second. With his free hand, Delverton shone his torch on to the cliff face, so that I could see my way down.

Connie lay prone on a wide shelf of rock, beyond which was a sheer drop, the sea foaming menacingly below. Her rucksack lay open beside her, one of her arms looped through it, and inside sat her handbag. I guessed her walking-pole had dropped into the sea.

31

I knelt beside her. "Connie," I whispered. "Can you hear me? It's Aidan Verney – from Harbour Heights."

As I repeated the words with more urgency, her eyes flickered open. I took hold of her wrist: the pulse was weak.

"A-Aidan?" She scarcely breathed my name. Gently, I took hold of her hand.

"You had a fall, Connie. But you're going to be all right. An ambulance is on its way. I'll wait here with you."

Her eyes sought mine. I couldn't read their message: anxiety, sadness; perhaps a warning? Her lips began to move, and I leaned closer in an effort to make out what she was trying to say.

"...Esley," she murmured. "Oh no...poor Will..." Her eyes closed, and her head lolled to one side.

7

I hoped she'd simply lost consciousness. There was still the faint flickering of her pulse, but I'd had no experience of these situations and was frightened to move her.

Delverton's head loomed into view above me. "You all right down there, Aidan? What's up? She trying to say something?"

"I couldn't make out the words," I mumbled, as much to myself as to him. "She's lost consciousness again. We badly need that ambulance."

It seemed as if it was taking forever. But Edward had had to make his way in the dark back to the Manor, and the ambulance would have had to come round by road from Leesbourne. I crouched there, patiently holding Connie's hand, conscious of Delverton pacing restlessly on the path above.

We heard the chilling whoop of the siren long before the bump of wheels on the rough track. Delverton hurried along to hail the ambulance crew, while I scrambled back to allow them room to get down and hoist Connie up on a stretcher.

Edward had returned from the Manor, and Holly came running down the track in the wake of the ambulance. We all stood aside, as the crew went about their work. I observed the pale faces and tense expressions of my companions and doubted I looked any different.

As, finally, the men brought Connie up from the ledge, another vehicle bounced down the track and halted beside the ambulance. It was a blue and white Panda car, from which a portly policeman heaved himself out and came over to us.

"Mrs Bayldon phoned me," he explained. "Bob Curtis, the Paxham constable. She said she'd gathered this poor lady had fallen while out rambling."

Everyone else seemed to have been struck dumb, their gazes drawn to the careful progress of the stretcher, so I answered for them. "Yes, we believe that's what happened."

"And you all know the lady?"

"Holly, Mr Delverton and I are all from the hotel where she's staying – Harbour Heights," I replied. "Mr Hambling joined us to help look for her. Her name's Miss Instow, Constance Instow, from London."

Curtis jerked a thumb towards the ambulance, into which the two men were installing the stretcher. "They'll be taking her to Leesbourne General," he said. "Do you mind going along with them, Mr -?"

"Verney. Aidan Verney. Certainly, I'll go."

"That's good of you, sir. I'll run your friends back into Paxham, then come along and join you at the hospital."

I thanked him and made to move towards the ambulance but was stalled by a tug on my sleeve. Holly was looking up at me imploringly, her eyes moist.

"Do you think she'll be all right, Aidan?"

I tried to be reassuring, to disguise my growing anxiety.

"Difficult to say, Holly. Go back to the hotel and let Miss Neale know. I'll phone when there's any news."

"All right." She lingered, her fingers still clutching my sleeve. I had to fight the urge to put my arm around her, for it seemed to me she was in need of consolation, perhaps not entirely due to her sadness over Connie's accident.

But then Edward called her name, and we looked up to see him waving her over to the Panda car. PC Curtis had taken charge of Connie's rucksack and was installing it in the boot, while Delverton waited beside him, hands in his trouser pockets. He seemed impatient to get away.

Holly joined them, and I got into the back of the ambulance to sit across from the stretcher. On our way back up the track, the ambulanceman sitting beside Connie's prone figure asked me some questions about her, and I answered as best I could: her name, where she was staying, where she lived, roughly how old she must be.

"I'm puzzled that she should have fallen," I added. "She was an experienced walker and would have known to keep well clear of the cliff edge."

The ambulanceman shrugged. "She might have spotted something out at sea which caught her eye, forgot for the moment where she was and missed her footing. I've known it happen. Lucky that shelf broke her fall, otherwise she'd never have survived the drop."

I found myself echoing Holly's question. "Do you think she'll be all right?"

The man grimaced. "Hard to say. She's elderly, there's the shock of the fall and everything, and the possibility of internal bleeding. They'll do all they can, I promise you."

I thanked him, and silence set in, the blare of the siren discouraging further conversation, as the ambulance tore along the main road. Once at the hospital, I watched as they transferred Connie to a gurney and took her inside. Her eyes were closed, and I couldn't help wondering if they'd ever open again.

Tears pricking at my eyes, I was shown to a small, square waiting room, its four walls lined with plastic chairs, a table in the middle with haphazard piles of dog-eared magazines, and an ashtray holding a pyramid of cigarette stubs.

After a while, I was joined by the Paxham constable. I soon warmed to PC Curtis, a bald, mountainous man, close to retirement, whose cosy Devonshire accent set me at ease. He asked questions about myself, nothing intrusive, and talked about Paxham, where he'd been the police presence for almost twenty years. I told him what little I knew about Connie and repeated my conviction that, as an experienced walker, she'd have taken care not to have strayed too close to the edge.

Before Curtis could comment, a doctor appeared in the doorway. He looked grim, and I felt with a start that he bore no good news.

He told us that Connie had died without regaining consciousness: the shock of the fall had put too much strain on her heart. He offered his condolences.

I battled to keep my tears at bay and sat with my head bowed. PC Curtis, clearly used to such situations, remained silent, giving me time to gather myself.

"She talked of a brother," I said at last. "He'll have to be informed."

"I've got her handbag and rucksack in the car," he assured me. "Should be an address in there somewhere. I'll take care of it."

"I ought to get back and let Miss Neale know." I decided against phoning: it'd be too impersonal, and I was sure Eleanor would be upset enough in any case.

"Let me run you back," PC Curtis offered. "Then I'll come and sort things out here. Poor lady. One slip is all it takes. She's not the first and won't be the last."

He dropped me off at Harbour Heights, promising to call round the next morning. Eleanor and Holly were waiting in the darkened lounge, the dregs of long-finished cocoa in mugs on the table before them. I didn't need to speak; they could tell what news I brought from the look on my face. Holly burst into tears, while Eleanor, dry-eyed but no less saddened, went and made me cocoa. I had no appetite for the dinner she'd kept by for me. It would have reminded me of the two dinners I'd eaten sitting alongside Connie. I might not have known her for long but had liked her and knew I'd miss her company.

"Mr Delverton's at the pub," Eleanor said scornfully. "Reckoned he needed a stiff drink for the shock. Good an excuse as any, I suppose."

We sat in gloomy silence as I drank my cocoa and related what PC Curtis had said. As I made my weary way up to bed, I thought again about Connie's accident.

The ambulanceman's words came back to me: *"One slip is all it takes."*

So, that was it: an accident. But then I recalled the previous evening: Connie, sitting in the lounge, staring after the departing Delverton. *"Surely – not the two of them?"*

I wondered what she'd meant by that?

8

PC Curtis called at Harbour Heights the following morning, just as I was finishing breakfast. Eleanor had informed Misses Gibbs and Moriarty of Connie's death, when they'd come downstairs. Both ladies looked shaken and expressed their condolences.

Tony Delverton arrived, seeming preoccupied. It might have been that his excesses of the previous night had caught up with him. He breakfasted on toast and black coffee and scarcely appeared to notice Holly, who'd mustered up the courage to serve him.

Curtis was chatting with Eleanor at the reception desk, when I emerged from the dining room. Finishing the coffee she'd poured for him, he informed us that there would have to be an inquest, although the hospital seemed satisfied that Connie had died of heart failure as a result of her fall. She'd lived in Blackheath in South London and, according to her address book, her brother lived nearby in Bermondsey.

"I've already contacted him," Curtis said. "The poor chap sounded devastated. He's heading down here by train – should arrive in Paxham on the three-thirty."

"I'd like to be there to meet him," I volunteered spontaneously, moved by the sudden thought that I'd be doing it for Connie.

Bob Curtis grinned. "I was about to ask if you'd accompany me, Mr Verney."

"And we'll put him up here," Eleanor cut in briskly. "It's the least we can do. He'll need to sort through her things. Oh, poor Miss Instow!"

So it was, that when the London train drew in to Paxham station that afternoon, PC Curtis and I were on hand to intercept the solitary passenger stepping down on to the platform.

He looked to be in his sixties, quite short and slight, with grey hair and a toothbrush moustache. He carried an ancient carpetbag and looked dapper in maroon blazer, beige flannels and brogues. But he looked downcast too, shaking hands solemnly as Curtis introduced us.

"Billy Instow, gentlemen. Thanks for coming to meet me." He shook his head sadly. "My, this is a bad business."

Curtis explained that we'd check him in at Harbour Heights, before driving him to the hospital, where he could formally identify his sister and pick up her belongings.

I sat next to him in the back of the police car, as we left the station. Billy Instow tried to remain stoical, but I could tell it was all he could do to hold back his tears.

"Poor Con. She was an amazing woman. Boundless energy. Served as a district nurse, y'know, for many years. Even in retirement, she helped down at the Seamen's Haven and was forever involved with her church and with never a thought for herself. God knows she was a better sister than I deserved."

"She was worried about you," I said. "Her last words were 'poor Will'. She must have meant you."

Instow smiled wryly. "Y'know, she always would call me Will. I'm Billy to everyone else, always have been. I was a wayward younger brother, my boy. She might have worried over worthier causes than me."

At Harbour Heights, Eleanor and Holly made Billy Instow welcome, sitting in the lounge with him, PC Curtis and myself over tea and biscuits. Afterwards, the constable drove him to Leesbourne hospital, later bringing him back with the effects Connie had had with her at the time of her fall.

The rucksack contained a map, hat, sunglasses and the remains of a packed lunch. I was present when Billy tipped out the contents of his sister's handbag. He was looking for her address book, as he wanted to send a telegram to the minister of her local church.

The address book and a purse were there, but I felt something was missing. It wasn't until later that evening that I remembered what it was: the crumpled photograph, which had fallen out two nights before and which I'd picked up and handed back. I hadn't given it a glance at the time, because that would have been impolite. I wondered what might have happened to it.

Billy Instow joined us for dinner and insisted on providing a glass of wine for everyone to thank us for our kindness, and also as a tribute to his sister. Eleanor Neale, a teetotaller, didn't altogether approve, but she felt sorry for Billy and generously stretched a point. Holly was despatched to the village supermarket and returned with two bottles. The ladies, Delverton, Holly and I all accepted a glass, while Billy polished off the rest. The wine lent him a false cheerfulness, a veneer which, I suspected, might collapse at any moment. Because of that, I decided to limit the conversation to mundane matters but was spared the effort, as Billy wittered on about nothing in particular, in an attempt to keep his spirits up.

Eleanor had brought three tables together, so that everyone could feel included. I felt obliged to Delverton, who took up the conversation with Billy. Both men were Londoners born and bred, so they had much in common, exchanging reminiscences of the war years, and how the city's landscape had changed in the decades which had followed.

The ladies chatted away with Eleanor about places they'd visited on what I'd gathered had been a month-long tour along the south coast.

This left me with Holly. She'd been sitting next to Eleanor but hadn't been much involved in the conversation. I was in the same position with Billy and Delverton and, with a shy smile, she'd come round the tables and taken the chair next to mine.

She still seemed a little subdued. Certainly, like me, she was sad about Connie, but I was sure that wasn't the whole reason. I believed something was troubling her and longed for the courage and opportunity to ask what it was. That time, with five other people in close proximity, wasn't now.

Our conversation remained on a superficial level. We talked of Paxham, ground which we'd mostly covered already, and she asked me about where I lived, an area in rural Oxfordshire, which she didn't know at all, and what sort of work I did. My replies were standard: I didn't divulge the nature of my illness, nor mention the break-up with Diana. By the same token, Holly gave away very little about her life before Paxham. Her mother was dead, and she'd never known her father. She'd left school at fifteen and had worked in a succession of cafés and pubs. However, I felt that we'd succeeded in establishing a bond between us, even if it was tenuous.

With the meal over and the wine finished, Holly helped Eleanor clear away. Delverton went off to the Lobster Pot, and the ladies ventured out for a slightly unsteady evening stroll. I accompanied Billy to the lounge, where I persuaded Holly to feed him several cups of strong coffee.

Billy hadn't stopped talking, delaying the inevitable. I learned that Connie had retired five years previously, having served as a district nurse in Deptford throughout the war and for another twenty years to follow.

"Even then she couldn't leave well alone. Nursing was in her blood. She helped out at an old people's home – blimey, some of 'em were younger than her! – and at the Seamen's Haven in Rotherhithe. Then, for years, she organised the Women's Bright Hour at her church. Phew! Wish I'd had her energy."

I asked him what he'd done for a living?

Billy took a noisy slurp of coffee. "Oh, I'm still working, my boy, if you can call it that. I'm a musician, you see, a pianist mainly, and also the black sheep of the family. Our dad blew a fuse when I told him I'd joined a jazz band. He never reckoned much to it at all. But I played under some of the great bandleaders: Geraldo, Joe Loss, Harry Roy. And some of those songbirds I played for – well, it reads like a who's who: Vera Lynn, Gracie Fields, Anne Shelton, Valerie Kaye. 'Course, during the war, I toured with ENSA: France, North Africa, playing the London clubs and dodging the bombs. Crikey, we were in the front line right enough, during the Blitz. And quite a few never made it through."

I had to smile at the image of Billy at a piano, complete with straw boater, ready smile and mischievous, sparkling eyes. But he was a long way from that now. He sighed.

"Well, I came out of it all right. But as for poor Con, she always was fretting over and looking out for me. Ah, she had a good heart. We lost our mum early on, see, and Con more or less brought me up."

"She never married, did she?" I put in. "Because the other night before she -, well, she mentioned a name. I couldn't catch it properly, but it sounded something like 'Esley'."

"Hhmm." Billy lapsed into thought. "Couldn't have been Lesley, could it? Somebody's surname? There was some bloke just before the war – nearest Con ever came to marriage. I think his surname could have been Lesley. Anyhow, as I recall, the poor blighter copped it in the Blitz. He was an air raid warden or some such. Con was very cut up." He stifled a belch. "I'll ponder that some more, my boy. Can't seem to think straight for the moment. Must've been something in that coffee..."

It was getting late. The ladies had returned and gone up to their room long ago, looking in at Billy with twinkly waves. Eleanor and Holly came into the lounge with their bedtime cocoa and offered us some.

Billy stood up unsteadily, and I arose with him, a supporting hand at his elbow. "Ladies," he announced flamboyantly. "Your hospitality has been tremendous, and I thank you from the bottom of my heart. But I should get out from under your feet while I can still walk." He blundered over to a startled Holly, seized her hand and kissed it. "Ah! Would I were forty years younger!"

He repeated the gesture with a blushing Eleanor. "Miss Neale, it's a mystery to me how you can have reached the age of thirty and not have been claimed. And Aidan -" Here I feared for the moment that I was about to receive the same treatment, but Billy merely offered his hand and shook mine warmly. "Thank you, my dear young man, for your company. And now, I bid you all goodnight."

He then flung open the nearest door and walked into a broom cupboard. Holly stifled a laugh, and, between us, we rescued him and escorted him up to his room; while Eleanor, her face scarlet, stood at the foot of the stairs, fondly shaking her head.

"Oh, he's a caution, and no mistake! Goodness me, what a charmer!"

9

Eleanor, Holly and I accompanied a once more subdued Billy Instow to the inquest in Leesbourne. After taking account of the evidence, the coroner brought in a verdict of accidental death.

We helped Billy arrange for his sister's body to be taken back to Blackheath, where her minister had agreed to conduct a private funeral.

"A few lusty hymns, that's all she'd ask," Billy said tearfully. "Our Con was a decent soul and never one to want a fuss made over her."

Much later that day, he collected up her few belongings and took his leave; but not before creating a scene in reception.

Eleanor flatly refused to take payment for his board and lodging, although Billy firmly insisted on paying his way. I was worried for a while that things might escalate into a full-scale argument. Finally, however, with Holly, Gibbs, Moriarty and I standing around as awestruck spectators, the protagonists relented, and Eleanor agreed to let him pay half the bill. Billy then sealed the deal by reaching across the desk and planting a smacking kiss on his hostess's cheek. Eleanor blushed, the ladies simpered, Holly giggled, and with an outrageous farewell to them all, he strode away, while I followed bemusedly in his wake.

"You know, Aidan," Billy declared, as I caught up with him and we headed towards the station. "You've been a real tonic and comfort to me, this past day or so. Sorry if I made a bit of a fool of myself last night, but it was my way of coping with the – the bad news. I understand you've not been well and hope things improve for you. Still," he flashed me a wicked grin, "I'm sure little Holly'll be a great help to you in that respect."

I stared at him in amazement. *"Holly?"*

"Oh, she's sweet on you and no mistake, young man. Take it from one who knows. And my good wishes go with you. She's a lovely little girl."

For several moments, I was struck dumb. I think Billy interpreted my silence as unwillingness to pursue the subject, and he made no further comment.

Arrived at the station, we exchanged addresses, and Billy invited me to drop in at his flat sooner rather than later, because he'd enjoyed my company so much.

His train came in, and I waved him off until he was out of sight. I dawdled back to Harbour Heights, feeling lifted by his words and friendliness and pondering the question of Holly. I liked her and I think she liked me. But I hadn't read anything more into that.

Most days, since I'd finished my treatment, I'd awoken feeling sorry for myself: no Diana, no job and possibly, before long, no life. However, I felt a little different the next morning, buoyed by Billy's comment about Holly, certainly. But that wasn't all.

I awoke with some sort of purpose. I'd not known Connie Instow for long but believed her to have been a good and compassionate person. As I recalled our first meeting in the harbour chapel, I got dressed and went down there early, lit a candle and knelt and prayed that she was now at peace. I examined the plaque, found Georgie Kell's name on it and felt sad for the young life snatched away; sad, too, for the woman who'd known and mourned him.

I felt somehow that I owed Connie a debt. I wasn't sure what it was, but something was nagging at me, trying to suggest that she might not have slipped and fallen. If that had been the case, the starting point might be the ferry sinking in which Georgie and nineteen others had died.

I mentioned my interest in the tragedy to Holly, when she served me at breakfast. She thought the village library would be worth a visit, as it kept archive copies of the *Leesbourne Gazette.* She offered to take me along there, if I'd wait until she'd finished the washing-up.

I hung around in reception, until she burst through the kitchen's swing door, apron-less in blue skirt and red tank-top. Eleanor glanced up from her book-keeping, switching a crafty glance between the two of us.

"You both off together, then?" Her eyes held a twinkle. I bumbled around for a reply, but Holly beat me to it.

"Just showing him the library, Miss Neale." She was sounding perky this morning.

"And then back here to tidy those rooms," Eleanor reminded her. "So, don't be long."

"Of course not, Miss Neale." There was a trace of indignation in the reply. Eleanor's lips twitched in a knowing little smile, as I followed Holly out.

The library was housed in the two front rooms of a stately Georgian house in Paxham High Street. Holly explained to the librarian what I was looking for, and he took us over to a far corner of the room, where the *Gazette* archives were shelved in heavy leather binders, five years to each volume. I helped him lift out the relevant one and plump it down on to a nearby table, the three of us coughing in the cloud of dust stirred up by this action. The librarian returned to his task of coding and recording several piles of recent acquisitions, and Holly said she ought to return to the hotel and carry out her chores. She promised to be back within the hour to see how I'd got on.

The *Leesbourne Belle* had been a foot passenger ferry crossing the mouth of the estuary between Leesbourne and Paxham several times a day. On the afternoon of 21st of May 1949, a storm was in the offing, and the ferry's captain, Abel Hart, a Paxham man who'd served in the Royal Navy in World War One, had set off from Leesbourne on the twenty-minute journey at five p.m.

The weather rapidly worsened, with waves tossing the little boat from side to side. But Hart was an experienced sailor and would have expected to make port without much difficulty, once they'd swung into the lee of Paxham harbour.

What he couldn't have foreseen, however, was that a fishing trawler had broken from its moorings and, as the *Belle* turned into the harbour, was driven alongside to clatter into the ferry amidships.

The *Belle* was an elderly vessel, and later inspection of the wreckage found evidence of rusting along both sides. It was holed by the lurching trawler and began to list badly. There was one dinghy on aboard, and Hart's two deckhands lowered it into the water, while the captain fought to right the boat.

Panic ensued, to the effect that people clambered frantically into the dinghy and almost capsized it. A number of passengers ended up in the water.

The whole incident had been witnessed by horrified spectators on the quay. An urgent call went out to the Leesbourne lifeboat, and several fishing boats put out from Paxham harbour.

These boats were first on the scene, but the rescuers couldn't prevent the loss of twenty lives, including that of Abel Hart, who went down with his boat. Listed among the dead was Madeleine Hambling, only daughter of Colonel and Mrs Bayldon of Paxham Manor. Mrs Hambling's five-year-old son was rescued, thanks to the bravery of Paxham fisherman James Neale, who was responsible for saving the lives of several passengers.

Later editions of the *Gazette* listed the names of those who'd perished, as well as testimonies from several survivors and an account of the inquest, where a verdict of accidental death was brought in. Other vessels had broken away from their moorings owing to the force of the storm, and several of these had suffered damage. It was generally felt that the fate of the *Leesbourne Belle* was a tragic misfortune.

Holly arrived back just as I was helping the librarian return the heavy binder to its accustomed place. I thanked him and followed Holly out into the street, where we met Edward Hambling striding across the road to meet us. He looked in a bad mood, scowling at me as if I had no right to be there and rudely addressing Holly.

"I thought you were meeting me at the Church Hall," he said gruffly. "I went to Harbour Heights when you didn't turn up and was told you'd come here."

"Well, I thought you said twelve o'clock," Holly replied defiantly. "And it's only just gone eleven-thirty now."

"I actually said eleven." Edward's tone was contemptuous, and his cheeks had turned pink. "Obviously you've forgotten." He shot me an unfriendly glance, which I pretended not to notice.

Quite frankly, the Edward-Holly situation puzzled me. I couldn't understand her interest in him. He was boorish and ill-mannered towards her, clearly considering himself a cut above.

Holly had turned to me, not bothering to argue any further. "Edward's giving a piano recital at the Church Hall this evening. I promised to go along with him this morning. I'm selling tickets at the door, and he's going to show me what I need to do. In fact -," she brightened suddenly, "why don't you come along at seven-thirty? It'll be good to see a friendly face."

Edward hadn't noticed what had obviously been a tilt at him. He was trying hard to work his constipated expression into a smile, aimed at me. "Yes, it would be good to have some more support."

"Thanks," I replied. "I'd love to." As with my sketching, I found listening to classical music therapeutic after my illness. Although I was aware that, in agreeing to attend, I was doing it more for Holly than for him or myself.

"The ladies from the hotel said that they'd come too," Holly added. She seemed glad that I'd accepted the invitation. "At this rate, it'll be a sell-out."

Edward reddened a little again. He seemed to have a habit of colouring up easily. On this occasion, though, he was suitably flattered.

"Really, Holly. That's just Gran talking. In her inimitable way, she's ordered half the village to be there. We'd better be getting along. See you this evening, Mr Verney."

"Please," I protested. "Call me Aidan."

"Yes. Right. Come along, Holly."

He set off purposefully, and she watched him go. "Thanks, Aidan," she said. "At least that's put him in a better mood. I think he feels tense about the recital. He's not usually so rude. I'll see you later. Enjoy your afternoon."

"I will. See you." I watched her hurrying after him.

I returned to the hotel to collect my sketchpad and pencils. On my way out, I mentioned to Eleanor about that evening's concert.

"Oh, you too?" she trilled. "That's fine, Mr Verney. The ladies are going as well, so I'll serve dinner at six. I'm sure Mr Delverton won't mind." She arched her eyebrows. "It'll give him more drinking time at the Lobster Pot."

10

I didn't bother sketching that afternoon, instead walking on impulse out to the spot where Connie Instow had suffered her fatal fall. I felt somehow drawn back there, almost as if Connie herself was willing it.

There was, of course, nothing to discover. Seen in daylight, it was a lovely spot. Looking back past the ruins of St Audric's chapel, I had a view of Paxham nestling in its harbour, sunlight glinting off the roofs and windows. While out to sea, which was serene and blue, I could glimpse the cross-channel ferries travelling between Weymouth, the Channel Islands and the French coast. The path was badly eroded in places, and I could see how easy it might be to lose one's footing. Then why did I find myself being nudged by suspicion?

I couldn't help feeling disconsolate as I trudged back to Harbour Heights, where, after resting for a while, I washed, changed and went down to dinner. Misses Gibbs and Moriarty enthused about 'young Mr Hambling's' forthcoming recital, although I gathered that they'd never met him; while Tony Delverton, after exchanging perfunctory courtesies with everyone, sat alone and ate his dinner in silence. It seemed to me that he had something on his mind.

The evening was calm and pleasant, as I made my way through the narrow streets to the Church Hall. The sun had long sunk beneath the distant cliffs, leaving a faint orange stain on the darkening sky. Holly was seated behind a trestle table inside the doorway, selling tickets and giving out programmes for the performance. She looked pretty in a yellow dress with a cardigan draped around her shoulders. The addition of eye shadow, lipstick and blusher, although in no way overdone, made her seem slightly older than her years.

She greeted me with a smile and tried to wave me past without taking my money. But I insisted on paying and, chancing a look around as I dug my hand in my pocket, it occurred to me that it was just as well I had, for I was being closely observed.

The lady watching me had to be Ruth Bayldon. She was positioned a few yards away from the door, keeping a close eye on everyone and everything. She was dressed uncompromisingly in tweed skirt and jacket and looked formidable, with a stern, hawk-like face, thin lips compressed in an expression which seemed to err on the side of disapproval.

I took a seat in the empty back row and exchanged nods with her as I passed. I sensed she was still watching me as I sat down, but I dared not turn round.

Gibbs and Moriarty were installed halfway down on the opposite side of the aisle and each accorded me a dainty wave. People still trickled in, but Holly's prediction of a sell-out seemed fanciful. I counted less than forty people scattered around the hall on hard wooden chairs. The empty ones, having been set out in hope, numbered more than those which were occupied.

The hall, like so many of its kind, was bleak: bare floorboards and ragged drapes across the high sash windows. A grand piano stood on a dais below a redundant stage, across which was drawn an ancient red velvet curtain.

I turned on hearing the clatter of footsteps behind me. Ruth Bayldon's voice gushed alarmingly. "Oh, how *lovely* to see you! I'm so glad you could come."

She'd almost run to the doorway to greet a tall, angular woman, who was smiling back at her condescendingly. Behind her, grinning vacuously, stood a clergyman who, I guessed, was the local vicar, short and with a red face topped by a swirl of white hair which reminded me of whipped cream.

I caught snatches of Ruth Bayldon's voice. "Oh, don't worry about tickets...here are your programmes...yes, I'm *sure* more people will be along, some leave it so late, you know...oh, dear Edward has practised and practised, this is *such* a proud moment for him..."

Only a handful more people arrived, however, none receiving quite the enthusiastic welcome which had greeted the angular lady. They also had to pay for admission. I gathered from the deferential nods and smiles from some members of the audience that she was one of Paxham's richer residents.

It was after seven thirty-five when Holly, on stage-whispered instructions from Mrs Bayldon, closed the doors. The proud grandmother had ushered her two guests to seats in the front row and now seated herself regally beside them. Holly, with a diffident smile, slid on to a chair next to me.

A hush descended on the audience. At the front of the hall, a door which had been open a crack now swung back to reveal Edward Hambling. His hair was combed back and shone with Brylcreem, he wore a long jacket with tails, bow tie and highly polished black shoes, which squeaked as he made his way to the dais. The audience applauded politely, and Edward turned, bowed deeply, shot back his cuffs and took his place at the piano.

To my untrained ears, he played well. His programme included well-known pieces by Chopin, Debussy, Ravel and Satie, and in the main he performed confidently. It wasn't a flawless performance, as one or two mistakes crept in, each apparent from Edward's grimace. I could see from his dark expression that he was angry with himself.

More sustained applause greeted the end of the performance, the florid vicar among those feeling moved to demand an encore, to which Edward obliged with some lively Chopin.

Most of the audience drifted quietly away after that, although a few lingered. Edward remained at the piano, in conversation with an elderly man, whose suit and bow tie had seen better days. They shook hands, and the man departed, exchanging a nod with Mrs Bayldon on his way past. She appeared to have been waiting for him to go, for she straightaway summoned Edward to her side, hauling him into a discussion with the angular lady and the vicar.

By this time, Holly had gathered up the takings, unsold tickets and programmes and bundled it all into a large envelope.

"She won't be pleased," she confided to me. "They'll just about cover the hire of the hall and cost of the posters. I ought to introduce you, I suppose." She looked up with a pert grin. "I'm sure you won't hold it against me."

Ruth Bayldon kept the two of us waiting, not even according us a glance. Her guests had clearly enjoyed the recital, and Edward's face glowed beneath an avalanche of praise. They finally took their leave, the angular lady saying she looked forward to seeing them both shortly.

Holly took a hesitant pace forward and held out the envelope. "Everything's inside, Mrs Bayldon," quickly adding, before that lady could move away, "Oh, and this is Aidan – Aidan Verney. He's staying at Harbour Heights."

Ruth Bayldon eyed me critically. I'd tried my best, with a limited wardrobe, to look presentable. My jumper was relatively new, even if my best flares were a bit creased. I wondered what she saw and didn't suppose she was greatly taken with me: a pale, thin, gangling young man with mousy brown hair curling trendily over his slightly frayed collar. Nowhere near as correct as Edward, to be sure.

She nodded stiffly. "Mr Verney."

"Pleased to meet you, Mrs Bayldon."

She acknowledged the greeting with something which fell short of a smile and took the envelope from Holly with an irritable glance at her grandson. He'd been distracted by a furtive study of the girl's legs but now snapped to attention.

"That skirt's too short, miss," Ruth said waspishly. "You'll remember another time to dress properly for a respectable gathering like this."

"Sorry, Mrs Bayldon." Holly seemed cowed and looked away. I quickly changed the subject, complimenting Edward on his performance.

He thanked me uncertainly, hardly able to look me in the eyes. I wasn't sure what I'd done but felt it had to be on account of his grandmother's brooding presence. Edward turned back to the dais to collect up his scores, and Holly went with him, eager to escape Ruth Bayldon but at the same time abandoning me to her tender mercies. I couldn't blame her, however. She'd been embarrassed by that comment.

Mrs Bayldon skewered me with an irresistible stare. "Edward has told me of your interest in the *Leesbourne Belle* tragedy, Mr Verney," she tersely. "My dear daughter Madeleine lost her life that day. Time is supposed to heal, I wish it did."

I felt immediately guilty. Twenty-one years since it had happened, and the poor woman was still suffering from her loss. "I'm very sorry, Mrs Bayldon."

She met my apology with the faintest of nods. "Madeleine was a brave young woman," she went on. "Her priority had been to get Edward clear, but she died in an attempt to save another boy. The fisherman, Neale, pulled them out of the water; too late, sadly, for them both. He did, however, succeed in rescuing the boy's aunt." The last sentence was spoken disparagingly, as if Snowy had had no right to have done that.

But Mrs Bayldon hadn't finished with me yet. "Perhaps I might ask the reason for your interest in the tragedy?"

"It stemmed from a conversation I had with Miss Instow. She was a fellow guest at Harbour Heights. She'd once nursed the little boy who died: Georgie Kell.

"Ah, yes. She mentioned it when taking tea at the Manor with me. Poor Miss Instow. A decent woman, I believe; and, sadly, another tragic accident."

Edward had re-joined us, a bulging music case under his arm. Holly stood slightly behind him, as if hoping he'd obscure her from his grandmother's critical gaze.

"I believe George Kell and I were good friends, weren't we, Gran?" he piped up. "Weren't my mother and his aunt -?"

Ruth Bayldon shot him a frosty glance. "Thank you, Edward."

He stepped back a pace, suitably abashed, and his grandmother turned back to me, her thin lips rehearsing a smile, which I feared more than her scorn.

"Mr Verney, we must talk further, but Edward and I have a prior engagement momentarily. Perhaps you'd care to join us for dinner at the Manor tomorrow evening? Shall we say seven for seven-thirty?"

I had no option but to accept, even though the prospect filled me with dread. There had to be a reason for the invitation, however, and I didn't think that it was because Ruth Bayldon had warmed to my personality.

I thanked her politely and, her aim accomplished, she was dismissive.

"Until tomorrow, then, Mr Verney. Edward and I must go. Perhaps, Miss Tasker," her probing gaze fixed on Holly, "you'd switch off the lights and drop the catch on the door before you leave. No doubt Mr Verney will escort you back to the hotel?"

She swept off into the night, while Edward, with a pale smile and nod to Holly and me, trudged off in her wake, departing the scene of his evening's triumph.

11

We were last to leave, and Holly pulled the door up behind us. Far down the street, the shadowy figures of Ruth Bayldon and Edward were slowly being swallowed into the night.

Holly's gaze was drawn to them, and, for a while, she watched in silence. "It's stating the obvious," she said, "but old Granny B doesn't like me." Her tone was light, but I caught in it the hint of hurt. "Let's face it, I'm a bit common for her precious Edward. Not that he wants me around anyway. I'm not even sure he's interested in girls."

"Are you interested in him?" It was a question I'd been wanting to ask for some time.

She shrugged. "There's not that many young people in Paxham. I ran into him up on the coast path one day, soon after I arrived here. He's very withdrawn and difficult to get to know. I suppose I felt sorry for him. He's so under Mrs Bayldon's thumb."

That answered my first question, and I felt bold enough to ask another, which had also been bothering me.

"Holly, why did you come here?"

She looked at me keenly, seemed puzzled for a moment, then shrugged again. "I don't know, really. I wanted to get out of London. I found it stifling, wanted a change of scene, a change of air. There was nothing to keep me there. Come to that, why did you?"

I grinned feebly. "I don't know either. I saw the harbour from the train and just, well – got off. I'd been ill for several weeks and needed to get away, to feel at peace, try to regain some confidence – not that I've ever had much. I – well, I had a girlfriend. While I was ill, she met someone else. I've never felt lower, needed desperately to be lifted…"

"Oh, you poor thing." The spontaneity of her sympathy stunned me. Her hand came up and squeezed my arm but didn't linger. "I'm really sorry, Aidan. Bad things shouldn't happen to nice people."

"But they do, Holly. It's a fact of life." I thought of Connie Instow.

We'd slowly begun to walk on and lapsed into another silence. She was close beside me, and I wondered if I might take her hand but lacked the courage. Failing that, I had to break the silence.

"You coped well with everything tonight," I blurted out, thinking how Ruth Bayldon had needlessly embarrassed her.

She smiled mirthlessly. "Oh, I have my uses. Granny will be on the blower to Nelly first thing, politely requesting my presence in the Manor's kitchen tomorrow night for your slap-up meal. Doubt if *she* knows how to boil an egg." She flicked me a playful glance. "Can't get away from me, can you?"

"What makes you think I'd want to?"

The response was out almost before I'd realised, and I felt alarmed, in case I'd said the wrong thing. We'd turned into Harbour Street and were just a few yards from the hotel. I halted abruptly, rocked by what I'd said, even though I'd meant every word.

Holly stopped too, and we faced each other uncertainly. I reached out, took her hand and pulled her close, so that our faces were inches apart. Her eyes, wide and trusting, somehow seemed to hold a plea. We drew closer.

"I say, what's going on here, then?"

We hadn't heard the hotel door open, and Tony Delverton came barrelling down the steps. He lurched past us, a crooked smile on his face.

I dropped Holly's hand rather quickly. "We -er, we've just been to the piano recital," I bleated.

He laughed coarsely. "'Course you have, Aidan. I can see that. Well, I'm off to resume a duet at the Boatman, then down to the Lobster Pot." He winked at Holly, who looked intimidated. "You behave yourself now, like a good girl."

He swaggered off round the corner, leaving us staring helplessly at one another. Then she reached up, kissed my cheek and hurried up the steps to the hotel. I followed her in, trying to catch up with her, sure that she was heading straight for her room.

However, Eleanor Neale emerged from the lounge at that moment, and Holly had to pull up sharply to avoid a collision.

"Oh, hello, you two." Eleanor's sweeping gaze had lit upon us both in the same instant. "What a shame you just missed Mr Delverton."

"No, we didn't," I observed flatly, and a smile twitched on Holly's face as she looked back at me.

"Well, I'll tell you all about it in a minute." Eleanor was trying to suppress her excitement. "Come into the lounge, both of you, and I'll get you a coffee. The ladies are just finishing theirs."

I wondered if Holly might make an excuse and was glad when she didn't. She went through and sat down on the sofa across from the ladies, and I parked myself beside her.

Gibbs and Moriarty had enjoyed the recital immensely and gave us a full account of the programme, as if we hadn't been present ourselves. Eleanor served us coffee with an impatient grimace and an eye roll, which the ladies, fortunately, didn't witness.

Holly thanked them for their kind remarks and promised to pass them on when she next saw Edward. Finally, they finished their drinks and tootled off to bed.

Checking that the ladies hadn't lingered in reception, Eleanor drew her chair closer to us. "Here's a juicy titbit," she said gleefully. "Our Mr Delverton popped back not long ago, reeking of beer. He wanted to use the payphone, because the one in the pub wasn't all that private, with people always going past. He waited for me to make myself scarce; which I did, in a manner of speaking.

"Now, I'm pretty sure he was phoning that woman who was here the other day, the one he called Val. Oh, oozing charm he was, trying to get the right side of her, and not making much headway either. 'Course, would you believe it, the boy walked in then, wanting me to settle up for the week's papers, and by the time he was gone, Mr Delverton was off the phone, and it's my guess he got short shrift. Not one to give up easily, though, is he?

"Anyway, then he fell into conversation with me and sat at the bar in here with a light ale. Which reminds me, I must add it to his bill. Now, as he tells it, he's a property developer. He heard about Paxham from a friend, came down here and likes it so much he wants to buy some land to set up a caravan park. He asked me if them up at the Manor had any land they might want to sell. Edward ever say anything about that to you, Holly?"

Holly looked pensive. "Not in so many words, Miss Neale, although as the whole village knows, they're strapped for cash. There are a couple of fields behind the Manor, that they rent out for grazing. I get the feeling Edward would sell, but he wouldn't dare go over Mrs Bayldon's head."

Eleanor laughed harshly. "Can't see our Mr Delverton cutting any ice with her."

Holly threw me a wicked smile. "Aidan had the pleasure of meeting her earlier."

"And found she wasn't too pleased about my interest in the *Leesbourne Belle*," I replied ruefully. "But, having lost her daughter, I can understand how she feels."

"Oh, blimey!" At that moment, Holly put a hand to her mouth and leapt up. "I promised to change the ladies' pillowcases and forgot all about it!"

"Well, you'd better get up there and do it, before they settle down for the night," Eleanor said tartly, shaking her head as she watched the girl cross reception and dash up the stairs. Once Holly was out of sight, she turned to me.

"Forgive me for seeming inquisitive, Mr Verney. But you were down at the library this morning and, if I might make so bold as to ask, something seems to have fired your interest in the ferry sinking?"

"I suppose it was Miss Instow," I replied. "She saw a name on the memorial plaque in the harbour chapel, the name of someone she'd known."

"Would that be Georgie Kell?"

"Yes." I stared back in surprise. "How did you guess?"

Eleanor gave a prim, informed little smile. "Rumours, Mr Verney, rumours. I'll say no more, in case I say too much, but you'd do well to have a word with that brother of mine."

"Snowy?"

"Ah, so he's called. Always been Jim to me." She chuckled. "Our Mum never called him anything but James. My goodness, how he hated that! Anyway, you have a chat with him. He's one who can give you chapter and verse, because he was there that day in the thick of it. Him and them others saved a lot of lives, including Master Edward's. And you'd think her ladyship'd be grateful for that."

I said I'd seek out Snowy the next day, although I'd intended doing so in any case. It was getting late, and I wished Eleanor goodnight. I met Holly on the stairs, on her way down from sorting out the ladies.

"Er, goodnight, Holly."

"Goodnight, Aidan."

We hesitated opposite one another, not quite touching. But then Eleanor hove into view at the foot of the stairs, and we hurriedly went our separate ways.

12

I went down to the harbour after breakfast the next morning to seek out Snowy Neale. The fishermen had been out early and had long ago returned with their catch. Some were busy drying their nets and cleaning down their boats, while others sat in pairs along the quay, puffing on pipes and swapping tales.

Snowy was in the middle of hosing down the deck of a fishing boat, which bore the name *Annie Mae*. He looked up and recognised me right away.

"Ahoy there! You're the lad staying up at my sister's place, ain't you? Good to see you. Hop aboard!" He reached across a hand to help me over the side. "You're the artist, ain't you? Not doing any drawing this fine morning?"

"Maybe later on," I replied. "I really came down to have a word with you."

He didn't seem to hear me, as something had claimed his attention. "P'raps you should've brought your drawing pad," he chuckled. "'Cause here's something worth painting. You might call it 'Drunk & Disorderly'."

I looked round to see Tony Delverton strolling along the quay towards us. He sported a lightweight summer suit and a pair of shades. Several of the fishermen had noticed him, nudging one another and looking amused.

Delverton ignored them. "Morning, gents," he called out to us, as he drew nearer, his teeth bared in a raffish grin.

"How's your head this morning?" Snowy called back. "Surprised it's still on your shoulders." He nodded towards the pub along the quay. "They'll be open soon. P'raps you should call in for a snifter? Hair of the dog, you know?"

To me, there was nothing jovial in Delverton's expression, and I guessed that the shades masked eyes which didn't smile.

"Not for me, pal. Head's clear enough for business, and I'm keeping it that way. Although, tell you what, I might pop along there in a bit and serenade the lovely Bet while you're busy sorting out your nets."

Snowy's good humour evaporated. "And I'll thank you to keep your filthy mitts of her," he growled back.

Delverton met the other man's animosity with a shrug and ambled away. Snowy's gnarled face looked mean, as he watched him go.

"Ah, he had a lucky escape last night," he muttered. "Got himself in a right state in the Lobster there. Irene refused to serve him in the end, and then, blow me, at kicking-out time, he blundered over his own feet, and my mate just about stopped him from pitching in the harbour. If it had been down to me, I'd have let him get on with it."

"Miss Neale tells me he's looking to buy a field to set up a caravan park?" I remarked.

"Ah, so rumour has it," Snowy grumbled. "Blowed if I'd sell him any field. Could do without his type around here."

"Something about land belonging to the Manor?" I persisted.

"Aye, young Mr Hambling owns a bit of land left him by his mother. Dare say our chum might twist *him* round his finger, but you mark my words, her ladyship won't let him get his hands on it."

By now, Delverton was out of sight, having turned up one of the paths leading away from the quay. I presumed he was taking a morning constitutional to ensure that clear head. I told Snowy there was a matter I wanted his advice on. "Your sister thought you'd be able to give me some information?"

"Depends what about, lad," Snowy replied. "But if our Nell reckons it, then likely I can. I'm about finished here, and it's too early for the Lobster. Let's pop up to my cottage and have a brew, and you can tell me what it's all about."

A hundred yards or so up the hill from the quay stood three rows of terraced cottages, which I'd passed on my walk along the estuary the other day. Snowy's stood at the end of the first row. The stonework needed painting, and the path outside was littered with fishing tackle, but once inside, I felt the house had a lived-in feel. The furniture was worn but serviceable, the paintings and photographs on the walls, sideboard and mantelpiece a little yellow and faded, and the tiny kitchen cluttered. It seemed to lack a woman's touch, but I guessed it served the genial fisherman well enough.

Snowy brewed tea in a large earthenware pot, poured it into chipped Coronation mugs and led me back outside, where we sat on a sun-bleached bench, surrounded by more nets and pots, looking down over the sleepy harbour and the calm sea shimmering in golden sunlight.

"What's on your mind, then, lad?" Snowy asked, as he handed me a mug of tea.

I told him of my conversations with Connie Instow and how, through her, I'd become interested in the ferry tragedy. I'd read the local newspaper accounts, discovering that Snowy had been one of the rescuers that day.

"Miss Instow? That's the poor lady who died in a fall t'other day?"

"That's right. I first met her in the chapel along the quay. She was studying the memorial plaque and saw a name she knew. Georgie Kell. Miss Instow had known him and his mother during the war."

"Ah, yes." Snowy's face remained impassive, but his manner was suddenly guarded. He was staring down across the harbour but didn't seem focused on anything in particular. I couldn't help thinking I'd just crossed a boundary. Even so, I carried on warily.

"Er, I believe Georgie's aunt was rescued. Does she still live in Paxham?"

"I rescued her." The words tumbled out in a hushed whisper, and Snowy's shoulders slumped. He cast me the briefest glance, but it was enough to show me his pain. "Her name was Annie Midson," he croaked.

I immediately felt awful. "Snowy, I'm so sorry if I -?"

Generously, he waved the apology away, got to his feet and indicated to me to follow him back inside. As I did so, I recalled the name of his fishing boat: *Annie Mae*.

Once we'd returned to the little living room, Snowy pointed to one of the framed photographs on the mantelpiece: a golden-haired young woman in a calf-length frock. She sat on Paxham quay, hands folded in her lap and her pretty face beaming brightly at the camera.

"Just nineteen when that were taken," Snowy said solemnly. "Loveliest gal that ever lived, little Annie. We were at school in the village and growed up together, see. She lived in the next row up from here.

"There was I – I can see myself now – plucking up the courage to ask her to marry me. Ah, but I was too slow, lad, too slow by half, and that's always been the way with me. My good friend Ned got there afore me, and I bowed out graciously, 'cause I could see he was the one for Annie. Ned and me were schoolfriends too, y'see, best pals, both of us into the fishing trade at fourteen.

"The war came a few years on, and him and Annie was married by then. We went into the Merchant Navy together but got different postings, like. Poor Ned got killed when his convoy was torpedoed in the Atlantic in '42.

"I made it through the war and came back to offer Annie what comfort I could. She had an older sister, who'd lost her husband too. Her health was real bad – TB, I think – and the doctor in London reckoned she should get back down to the coast for a change of air. So, down she comes, with her little lad Georgie, to live with Annie.

"Her sister's condition got worse, and Annie worked to keep the three of 'em. My, but you had to admire that gal's spirit. She took in washing, ironing and sewing, and they scraped by. When I thought the time was right, I asked her. She let me down gently. See, there was no-one could take Ned's place.

"And once her poor sister was gone, Annie devoted herself to that little boy, loved him as if he'd been her own, worked her fingers to the bone for him. I can't help thinking, if only through having to make ends meet, whether she'd have eventually considered marrying again." He shook his head sadly, as he gazed through the window at the harbour. "Ah, but the ferry changed all that..."

13

"I shan't forget that day as long as I live." Snowy, standing at the window, was years away, seeing the harbour below not in its present tranquil setting, but how it had looked all those years ago, the savage swell of the sea buffeting the boats, causing them to hiccup violently on the water, yank fractiously at their moorings; and the sky above, dark, evil and brooding.

"I was on the quay as they come past afore it happened." His voice was mournful, echoing. I might not have been in the room. I wondered if he'd experienced many times like this, nothing and no-one to distract him, just himself, reliving the memories and sadness.

"Them two little lads were as like as two peas in a pod. Oh, laughing and tumbling about, they were. Might've been twins in their hooped T-shirts, khaki shorts and plimsolls. And the two women, Madeleine Hambling and Annie Midson, all fresh and smiling in their pretty summer frocks. Ah, they got a barrel-load of admiring glances from them of us along the quay.

"Madeleine Hambling was a sweet-natured woman, generous to a fault. Annie had told me she'd bought the clothes for Georgie, same as Edward's, 'cause Annie 'ud never have been able to afford it. But she'd made her swear never to let her mother get wind of it. And Annie. What could I say about Annie that I've never already said or thought over and over again? I wondered if either of 'em might ever remarry. Madeleine perhaps, except her mother 'ud insist on the right match, what with the first having been a general's son. But Annie?

"Well, if she did, I knew by then it wouldn't be to me. We'd had tea together just the week before, see, when Georgie had been up at the Manor playing Cowboys and Indians or some such, with young Edward. I'd asked her then and, God bless her, she'd let me down lightly; always kind-hearted, always gentle wi' me, great lummox that I am. I seen her take that glance at her husband's photo on the sideboard: Ned, tall and dark, wi' his boyish grin. And I had my answer. Ned had always been the only one.

"Them were my thoughts, as I watched the ferry chug past, with Abel Hart at the wheel. "That old wreck's been about longer than I have!" somebody called out. "What old wreck?" another wag answered. "Abel or the *Belle*?"" Snowy paused, chuckled mirthlessly. "I recall we all stood there laughing, five or six of us, saluting Abel on his way past. Ah, and he saluted us back right enough, but not in a polite manner.

"Well, we all shuffled off to the pub then and stayed all afternoon, quaffing pints and playing darts or dominoes, 'cause outside the rain started bucketing down, heavy squalls driving in off the sea and causing the boats to strain and heave at their moorings. And somebody – think it must've been Irene's dad, who ran the pub back then – wondered if Abel 'ud bring the *Belle* back in that storm. But we all agreed he probably would – he'd come through a whole lot worse than that in his Royal Navy days.

"After a bit, the rain eased, but then a gale sprang up, and the wind howled like a demon round the harbour. Suddenly, the pub door crashed open, and the harbourmaster almost fell in, water streaming off his oilskins. He bawled out that some trawler had broke off its moorings and was getting tossed all over the estuary, and there was the *Belle* on her way back from Leesbourne.

"As he finished speaking, there come the most fearful sound of a collision, and we heard these screams and shouts sounding feeble in that vicious gale. The harbourmaster barked to the landlord to get on the blower to the Leesbourne lifeboat, but by then four or five of us was running out on to the quay and heading for our boats."

He turned towards me a face gaunt with misery. *"Time is supposed to heal,"* Ruth Bayldon had said, only the previous evening. *"I wish it did"* The pain remained for Snowy Neale; and I felt for him in his suffering.

"I was the first one out," he went on. "Annie was foremost in my mind: the thought of her plunged into that turbulent sea spurred me into action. But there was them others too, as many as forty on that ferry, not to mention Mrs Hambling and the two young boys.

"My old boat was the *Snowstorm* in them days, and a couple of my mates followed me on. One of 'em – old Bert, it must have been – went straight to the wheelhouse, while I cast off. As we swung out into the harbour, we were well ahead of anyone else. I stood in the bow and peered through the driving rain. Some trawler had rammed into the ferry, and the *Belle* was listing badly. There were people in the water, crying out for help. Abel's two deckhands were lowering the dinghy, and people were scrambling to get into it almost afore it had hit the water, not far off capsizing it.

"There was nothing else for it, lad. I kicked off my boots and struggled into a lifejacket. I recall Bert looking at me as if I was mad, but I yelled back that I was going in and for him to take the boat alongside some of them floundering in the water. See, I was looking for the bright frocks of the two women, and I couldn't spot 'em in the dinghy or on the ferry's deck. They had to be in the water.

"I dived in, and I used to thank the good Lord every day that by some happy chance, I came upon Annie first. She was unconscious, and I dragged her back to the *Snowstorm*, where my mates hauled her aboard. It was only much later I learned that her,

Madeleine and the boys had been tossed off the starboard deck, when that blasted trawler had walloped into the *Belle's* port side.

"I went back in. I could make out the Leesbourne lifeboat approaching across the mouth of the estuary, but the *Belle* was already going down. Abel's deckhands had managed to launch the dinghy. They were clinging to its sides, and it was crammed with crying, frightened people.

"I heard someone call my name and glimpsed Madeleine Hambling not ten yards off. I saw no sign of the boys. I swam towards her, and only then did I notice she had one of 'em in tow. He looked unconscious, and Madeleine was close to hysterical. "Gone – under!" she yelled, her voice a screech, whipped away by the wind. "Must find him!"

"I took charge of the boy and, as the dinghy lunged closer, offloaded him into several pairs of willing hands. I swam back to where I'd seen Madeleine and, through the rain, could make out her struggling with t'other boy. They went under twice, afore I could get to 'em, and it struck me she must've been exhausted. I was labouring, too, and had to call on every ounce of strength I could muster to take firm hold of her and the boy. My lungs was bursting, and I was urging 'em to hang on, just hang on, but wasn't sure they could hear me.

"I was only just aware of the lifeboat lurching up close to us, and first the boy, then Madeleine, were hauled up into the boat. Somehow, I don't know how, I must've followed, and the next I knew was I was lying on my side on Paxham quay in a great puddle of water and feeling as sick as a dog.

"Somebody told me later I gasped Annie's name, afore I passed out again."

14

Snowy's shoulders slumped as he finished his tale, and I could tell that it had cost him dear. He stood at the window peering out across the harbour; but I was sure that all he could see were the mayhem and human tragedy of that storm-ravaged day twenty-one years before.

"They weren't able to revive Madeleine Hambling nor young Georgie," he said in a dull voice. "Twenty people died, all told, poor Abel Hart among them, God rest his brave soul. The ferry company was prosecuted, 'cause the insurance people reckoned the

Belle weren't seaworthy, and the weight of the fines they had to pay in compensation sent 'em to the wall. Not many of us lost any sleep over that, I can tell you. Nothing could bring back them as lost their lives. I was counted one of the lucky ones. I didn't feel so lucky, and nor do I now."

"I'm sorry," I said. My apology was heartfelt. Once more, my idle interest had caused an upset. I wasn't proud of that. And yet, an idea was stirring in my mind. Eleanor Neale had spoken of rumours. I began to ponder over what those rumours might be.

Snowy grinned sadly. "Not your fault, lad. Just that it won't ever go away." He sighed. "Poor Annie was ill in hospital for a while. Soon as she'd learned what had happened to little Georgie, all the life seemed to drain out of her.

"It was Colonel Bayldon took charge of the situation. He was a brick and no mistake. Sorted out the funerals of Georgie, Abel and one or two other locals. Annie wanted to go up to the chapel of rest to set eyes on the little lad one last time, but the Colonel strongly advised her against it. He reckoned it'd have upset her too much.

"Annie took the loss of the boy hard. She hadn't a soul left in the world. Her parents were long dead, her husband killed in the war, and her sister died soon after it. Poor lass went about in a daze. Some of the womenfolk took against her. They reckoned she was just playing on people's sympathy, else trying to hook herself somebody's man. Her ladyship up at the Manor was thought to be one of the main instigators, 'cause another rumour going the rounds was that Colonel Bayldon was getting too friendly-like. Annie was still a mighty good-looking woman, although the business had aged her. As it had the Bayldons, to be fair, losing their only child.

"You'd always find Annie up at Georgie's grave with fresh flowers most weeks, and a wreath at Christmas-time. After a while, though, she took to drink: gin and the like, ended up spending nearly every penny she had on it. People still tried to help her: Nell and me, and the colonel. But it wasn't three years after the tragedy that he found her at the bottom of her stairs with a broken neck. They said it was the drink as caused it: but to my mind, the ferry tragedy had claimed another victim."

I was about to commiserate further, when the click of the gate latch made us both look up. Snowy's face cleared of a sudden, and he winked at me. "My sourpuss sister," he grinned, then called out, "Mornin', our Nell."

Eleanor was having difficulty with the cottage door and, as I was nearest, I got up and opened it for her. She bobbed her head in thanks, as she staggered in carrying a plate covered with a napkin.

"What a gentleman you are, Mr Verney," she declared. "More than I can say for some. Here you are, our Jim. Take hold of this and put it in the oven to warm through tonight. Meat and potato pie. I was preparing one for dinner tonight and thought I might as well do one for you."

"That's kind of you, sister. And it's good of you to come out of your way to bring it. 'Course, you might have sent young Holly down with it. She'd brighten up the place no end." He leered at me. "And I shouldn't think Aidan 'ud have objected, either."

I immediately sensed my face colouring up, but fortunately Snowy's attention had been claimed by a timely harangue from his sister.

"She's young enough to be your daughter – granddaughter, nearly," Eleanor scolded. "Our Mum 'ud have a fit at the way you carry on. Here, you take this into your kitchen. I refuse to set foot in there, 'cause it's bound to look like a rubbish tip. In here's just as bad. You should get that woman friend of yours to tidy it up. Make a change from her doing herself up to the eyeballs all the time."

I wondered if Snowy might take umbrage at that, but he merely grinned. "Perhaps I should come along to chapel on Sunday, then," he said, throwing me a sly wink. "Repent all my sins."

"Huh, if you ever set foot in there, the whole congregation 'ud pass out at a stroke." She turned to me, that inquisitive glint in her eye. "I should imagine he's been telling you a tale or two, Mr Verney?"

"Yes, I've learned a lot," I replied. "Particularly about the way Colonel Bayldon helped out some of the villagers after the tragedy."

"Decent enough man, the colonel," Eleanor said. She glanced towards her brother, who was looking solemn. "Our Jim won't mind me saying this, I'm sure, but people did gossip a lot at the time over the amount of attention Colonel Bayldon showed Annie Midson."

"I already said," Snowy mumbled. "But Colonel felt guilty that young Edward had lived, and Annie's boy had died."

"Yes, I suppose he acted through natural Christian decency." Eleanor somehow managed to inject a note of doubt into her words. "Although I'm sure her ladyship didn't see it that way. Still, she was the one who gave Annie some work with the cleaning up at the Manor a year or so later, once they'd packed Edward off to boarding school. Managed to help her get back on her feet, like." She looked at her brother, who was gazing down at the floor. "Sadly, by that time the demon drink had taken hold."

"So, is that what you meant by rumours, Miss Neale?" I asked candidly. "The gossip about Annie and Colonel Bayldon?" I caught the furtive glance of conspiracy between brother and sister.

"The Bayldons weren't greatly liked," Snowy put in. "They were lord and lady of the Manor and didn't mind who knew it. The Colonel was a JP and on this and that committee, and some didn't like that; although, as I said before, he was all right and his daughter a chip off the old block. But his missus always was overbearing and putting on airs and graces, and folks didn't take kindly to it."

"Ruth Bayldon came from a good family, but they never had two ha'pennies to rub together," Eleanor added waspishly. "Though she never let that stop her queening it over everybody, and it don't stop her now."

"She took young Edward under her wing," Snowy went on, "and turned him into a milksop. Pretty little lass like Holly shows an interest in him, and all he can do is look down on her, just because his gran tells him she's not good enough. The Bayldons wrapped that boy in cotton wool from the minute he come out of hospital. Oh, I don't doubt they were relieved he survived, or that they were in shock after losing their daughter that way. Even so, our Nell's never forgiven 'em the slight…"

"What slight?" I asked, my interest fired.

"Our Mum." Eleanor looked nettled. "She was a qualified nurse, living right here in Paxham, near enough on their blinkin' doorstep. But no, when Master Edward was home and recovering at the Manor, the Bayldons brought in some woman from Leesbourne to tend to him, and her having to bike round from there each time, 'cause no-one 'ud trust to the ferry."

I frowned. "Surely, that was a bit odd?"

"I should say it was," Snowy continued. "But it didn't stop there. They reckoned Paxham school was too rough, so in come a private tutor to teach him at home,

63

till he reached his seventh birthday. Then he was off to boarding school. Poor little devil. Can't wonder at it, him turning out to be such a queer fish."

15

Eleanor Neale clapped her hands. "Enough gossiping for one day," she declared, "else I shall be getting a reputation. I've a hotel to run and standing here jawing won't help get the veg prepared."

It was a timely reminder for me. "Er, I'm afraid I'll be missing," I piped up. "I've been invited to dinner at the Manor."

Snowy chuckled. "Dare say that'll be bib and tucker, then?"

His sister snorted. "Not much chance of that. Oh, her ladyship rang before I came down here. All sweetness and light, she was. Could I possibly spare my young colleague to help cook the meal this evening? *Help?* I ask you! And you might take an educated guess as to where the apple pie'll have come from."

With that, she bade us good morning and set off back to Harbour Heights. I decided I ought to be going too and thanked Snowy for telling me all he had. "I really appreciate it. And I apologise for stirring up painful memories."

He nodded gloomily. "Aye, lad. There's some things you never forget."

"Perhaps I could stand you a drink?" From the cottage window, I could see a trickle of customers entering the Lobster Pot, and I felt it was the least I could do.

Snowy perked up a little. "That's right decent of you, lad. Tell you what, I'll introduce you to Clarence Darby. He's bound sure to be in there, never often misses popping in for a lunchtime sandwich and glass of wine." I looked at him blankly. It was a name I didn't know. "He was young Edward's private tutor all them years ago," Snowy explained.

He stored his pie in the larder, and we walked down to the pub. Bet was behind the bar and called out a welcome. If his recounting of the ferry tragedy had upset him in any way, Snowy quickly put it behind him, his weather-beaten features enlivened at the sight of the barmaid. I saw that Irene Pake, bringing plates of sandwiches through from the kitchen, was surveying them sullenly. She happened to catch my eye and nodded grudgingly, then turned away without answering as Snowy greeted her belatedly.

Bet pulled a pint of mild for Snowy and a small shandy for me, while he pointed out Clarence Darby. He sat alone in the farthest corner, fortifying himself with wine and a sandwich. He looked smart in blazer and flannels, his straw hat hung on the back of an adjacent chair, against which was propped a malacca cane. I recognised him right away as the man who'd been speaking to Edward following the previous evening's recital.

"Why the interest in Clarence?" Bet asked, as she placed our glasses in front of us.

"Aidan's interested in the *Leesbourne Belle* sinking," Snowy explained. "I told him about Colonel Bayldon's kindness to them who was affected by it, and the way him and his missus undertook bringing up young Edward. 'Course, they took on Clarence as the boy's tutor, soon after he come to Paxham. So, as we've been talking all around it, we wondered what observations Clarence might have. He got as close to the family as anyone at the time."

Bet gave Snowy's hand a reassuring pat. "It all happened long before I came here, but I know poor Snowy always regrets not having been able to save both boys. I heard they were such great friends, bless 'em, and *so* alike. You come over with me, Aidan. I can introduce you and pick up his empty plate and cutlery. Clarence likes nothing better than to sit and have a chat."

I'd noticed that Clarence Darby's glass was nearly empty and asked Bet if she'd refill it for him? She took payment from me and picked up the wine bottle from behind the bar, unlucky enough to be observed by Irene as she did so.

"Can you get along and serve down this end of the bar, Bet?" she snapped. "'Stead of standing around gossiping?"

"I'm doing Mr Darby a refill," Bet explained reasonably.

"Well, why don't you get on with it, then?"

Snowy raised a cautious eyebrow in my direction. "Sounds like somebody got out of bed the wrong side," he mumbled.

"Somebody always does," Bet groaned. Bottle in hand, she squeezed out from behind the bar.

I thanked Snowy and followed her. Looking back, I noticed that he'd quickly joined in a conversation with a small group of fishermen. Perhaps he'd realised that standing at the bar alone made him an easy target for Irene's current bad mood.

It was only then that I noticed Tony Delverton perched on a stool at the end of the bar, keeping a lively eye on Bet's progress across the floor. He seemed unaware that Irene Pake was scowling in his direction; but I supposed she scowled at everyone.

The moment Delverton looked round and saw her, he raised his almost empty glass. "'Nother pint of best, love," he called out. Irene stalked the length of the bar and snatched up the glass with unconcealed ill grace.

The elderly man at the corner table looked up in surprise, as Bet appeared beside him and replenished his glass.

"Ah, to what do I owe this pleasure?" he inquired.

Bet nodded at me. "This young man's staying at Harbour Heights, Clarence," she explained. "He's been listening to Snowy's tales, and Snowy pointed him in your direction. He's kindly bought you a refill, so, if you let me take that plate, I'm sure you won't mind spending a bit of time with him?"

"Indeed not," Clarence Darby agreed. "Take a seat, young man."

I offered my hand, as he bobbed up from his chair. "Aidan Verney, sir. Pleased to meet you." His grip was frail and, observing the long, tapered fingers, I assumed that he and Edward Hambling had music in common.

As I sat down opposite him, I noticed him appraising me shrewdly. "How long have you been staying in Paxham, Mr Verney?" he asked.

I explained that I'd been there a few days, taking a holiday and the sea air, as I was recovering from an illness.

He didn't press the issue, nodding sagely and raising his glass. "Then I wish you the very best of health, young man, and my grateful thanks." He spoke in a clipped, cultured voice, pleasing on the ear.

"I'm finding the sea air invigorating," I went on, "but listening to classical music is proving good therapy too. I was at Edward Hambling's recital yesterday evening and believe I saw you there?"

66

"That's right. And what did you think of his performance, Mr Verney?"

"Oh, please. Call me Aidan. I'm neither an expert nor a musician, but I thought he played well."

"He's certainly getting there. But it was a great pity that the audience was so sparse. He fared little better in Leesbourne back in the spring. I know he'll have been disappointed, but I can see he drives himself too hard. He's desperate to establish himself as a professional musician, a difficult enough task in itself."

"I only know Edward slightly. But he comes across as an emotional type."

"He's highly strung." Clarence shot me a searching glance. "I'm afraid his grandmother doesn't help. She can be very demanding."

"Do you know them well, Mr Darby?"

"Oh, yes." He took another sip of his wine, sat for a moment in thought. "Yes, since Edward was very small. I was employed for a while as his tutor and introduced him to the piano, along with other subjects."

Not for the first time that morning, I wondered where all this might be heading. Something was nagging me about the aftermath of the ferry sinking, in which one boy had died and another been saved. I needed to be alone to get my thoughts in some semblance of order.

The manner of Connie Instow's death was also troubling me, and for some reason I believed it might be at the nucleus of everything. She'd given me the impression of having been a careful sort of woman, added to which she'd been an experienced walker. Would she willingly have ventured so close to the edge of the cliff?

I'd only just met Clarence Darby but, from the evidence of the last few minutes, I believed him to be a straight talker and decided to share what was on my mind. I kept my voice low, not that there was anyone else close by, and the old man, sensing the need for confidentiality, leaned forward to better catch my words.

"I've been talking to Snowy Neale and his sister," I said. "They seemed to have felt put out that the Bayldons didn't employ their mother, who lived in Paxham, to nurse Edward after the tragedy."

Clarence Darby chuckled softly. "Oh, you mustn't blame the Bayldons. The woman was a notorious gossip, who would have delighted in spreading tittle-tattle about the family throughout the community. And I have to say that Miss Neale, for all that she has a generous heart, always likes to be in the know about everything."

"And your appointment as tutor, Mr Darby? Why did they distrust the local primary school?"

This might have been the point where Clarence told me to mind my own business, but I saw from his concentrated expression that my question was one he'd probably asked himself before.

"He'd been due to start there the following September," he replied. "And that had been his late mother's wish. But his grandparents decided not to send him there. He was a delicate child, and Ruth Bayldon told me at the time that she felt the school 'too rough'. The lad was emotionally scarred, which was unsurprising, having lost his mother in such dreadful circumstances. I could understand their reasoning, but my own opinion was that mixing with other children would be good for him rather than otherwise."

He sipped his wine and leaned closer, dropping his voice still further.

"I'm afraid I didn't state the case *too* forthrightly, as I wasn't in a position to do so. I'd left my post at a minor public school that spring and had come to Paxham for the sake of my health, with a view to getting by on offering private tuition.

"No, I accepted Roderick Bayldon's offer with alacrity and was glad I had, for Edward was a biddable pupil, quickly displaying an aptitude for music, as well as other subjects. However, within two years, they'd packed him off to Roderick's old boarding school. I'm amazed that he survived, but fortunately his love of music was his salvation, and he went on to study at the Royal College, where he acquitted himself reasonably well. His grandmother doesn't mean to hold him back, I'm sure, but she is his stumbling block. He needs to be allowed to mix with people of his own age and not worry too much about their social background."

I had to smile at the old tutor's wry observations. I hadn't reckoned him to be one to pull punches, and he hadn't disappointed.

"I've got the impression that the Bayldons were never well off," I went on. "So, how could they afford private tuition?"

"My fees were far from exorbitant," Clarence replied. "But in fact, Colonel Bayldon didn't have to part with a penny, as the bills were met by Edward's paternal grandfather. You may have heard of General Marcus Hambling?"

I shook my head.

"He was decorated in both World Wars," I was told, "although, tragically, both his sons perished in the last one. Edward is the general's sole beneficiary, although he tells me his grandfather's still going at almost ninety."

I remembered then that Edward had mentioned the general the other day, having just arrived back from paying him a visit.

Irene Pake called time in a voice which brooked no argument, and Clarence Darby finished his wine and pushed back his chair. As he got slowly to his feet, I passed him his hat and cane and thanked him for his time.

He smiled deprecatingly. "I'm just an old man who likes to talk," he said. "And I've enjoyed our chat. You must call by for a cup of tea or something stronger before you leave Paxham. I live in one of the bungalows at the top of the lane: 'Rose Revived'." He chuckled. "People often ask me who Rose is. I haven't a clue."

We wished each other a good afternoon, and Clarence toddled away. I took our empty glasses back to the bar, getting in return a cheery "Thanks, lovey," from Bet and a curt nod from Irene, who was pointedly standing over the grinning Delverton, in an effort to persuade him to drink up and leave.

16

"Hey! Wait up there!"

I hadn't got far along the quay, when I turned to see Tony Delverton scurrying after me. With his lightweight summer suit and bronzed face, he might have passed for thirty-something from a distance. But as he drew closer, I could make out the crinkled skin around his eyes, the lined forehead, and in his haste, he was panting audibly.

"Hold up, Aidan. What's the rush?"

I waited, rewarded with a blast of beery breath, as he lurched to a halt. My initial instinct was to distrust his motives, for there was a predatory look about his broad smile.

"P'raps you didn't clock me at the end of the bar just now, Aidan? But you seemed well in with Snowy Neale and deep in discussion with that old sweetheart Clarence. You heading back to the hotel now?"

I admitted cautiously that I was. Afraid that he might suggest a drink in the lounge, I added that I intended being quickly off again. We started up the slope towards Harbour Heights, and I wasn't left to wonder too long as to why Delverton was so keen to keep my company.

"Interesting tale they have to tell, don't you reckon?"

"Sorry?"

The smile stretched wider, but I sensed irritation behind it.

"Snowy and Clarence, mate. Listen, p'raps you and me ought to meet over dinner tonight. Kind of pool our resources and see if we can't help one another out?"

"I'm afraid I'm out for dinner tonight," I replied, without much trace of apology. "And besides, I'm not quite sure what you're driving at?"

There was truth in my last sentence. Had Delverton been conversing with Snowy and Clarence along the same lines as I'd done that morning? If so, what might be his reasons for getting involved?

The smile remained, but his eyes were narrow and vicious. What sort of sinister game was he playing? "Ah, I see. You're just being cagey, aren't you? But I can tell you've got my drift all right. All I ask is for you to give my little suggestion some thought, eh? Then we'll talk about it some more."

We'd reached the top of the slope, just across the road from the hotel. Delverton turned to cast an admiring look over the harbour, breathed in and expelled a lungful of air. I may well have irritated him minutes earlier, but his expansive smile and complacent manner annoyed me now. I doubted that he was smiling inside.

"Nice part of the world, this," he went on. "And not a million miles from dirty old London. Been thinking of getting a flat or log cabin or something and come down and end my days here. I'll give it some thought."

I grinned back, but only because I'd just hit on a way to test the validity of that infuriating smile.

"Yes, Miss Instow liked it too," I said.

"Who?" I'd distracted him. "Oh, yeah, right. The poor mare who fell off the cliff. She seemed a decent sort. Tragic, that. But accidents do happen. Ah, well, best push on. They say time's money and they're not wrong."

I followed him across the road and up the steps to the hotel's open door.

"Mr Delverton?"

He looked over his shoulder. "Call me Tony, son."

"Right. Tony – did you know Miss Instow? Before you met her in Paxham, I mean?"

I asked the question in a matter-of-fact way, but it had a startling effect on him. His features tightened, and he was immediately on the defensive. His smug smile was history.

"I never clapped eyes on her before. Why d'you ask?"

I shrugged effortlessly. "Just your London backgrounds, I suppose. She'd lived there all her life."

There seemed to be a hint of pity in his expression. "London's a heck of a big place, old mate, and I've covered a lot of it in my time. Never run across your Miss Instow before I met her right here in this hotel just the other day."

Delverton turned, reached the reception desk in three strides, snatched his key off the rack and disappeared rapidly up the stairs.

I watched him go, recalling those same words I'd spoken to Connie Instow earlier in the week: "London's a big place." And she'd replied: "But it's a small world."

Small enough that she and Delverton might have crossed paths before they'd arrived in Paxham?

And if that had been the case, might he for some reason have wanted her out of the way?

*

71

I went upstairs to rest a while, after which I collected my things to go off sketching for the remainder of the afternoon. I was about to set off, when there came a knock on the door. Eleanor Neale stood outside, looking a little flustered.

"Phone call for you in reception, Mr Verney," she announced. "It's that brother of Miss Instow's. Honestly, that man *is* a caution."

I went down to take the call. Eleanor followed and remained in close proximity, straightening the leaflets in the rack and trying to give the impression of someone not eavesdropping on a private conversation.

Billy Instow came across as the pleasant, breezy person I'd reckoned him to be, now that his initial wave of grief over his sister's death had passed. I'd almost forgotten about our conversation concerning the man with whom Connie had once been friendly.

"I was right about him having been an air raid warden," Billy chirped. "His name was Joe Lessley, and it seems they met at her church. He was a fair bit older than Con, and the poor blighter copped it in the Blitz. But the more I think of it, Aidan, the more I doubt whether it was him she was referring to when – y'know, when *it* happened. I mean, if it was him, why didn't she call him Joe? She must've known him as Joe, even if they were always formal with one another, shaking hands when they said goodnight, and what have you?"

Billy and I talked for a while about nothing in particular and ended with my promise to look him up when I next visited London and his request for me not to leave that too long.

Eleanor loomed back into view, as I replaced the receiver, her politely inquiring expression inviting me to divulge the subject of my conversation. She was able to tell from my tight smile that it wasn't going to happen, and I picked up my things, thanked her and walked away.

"Do enjoy dinner at the Manor this evening, Mr Verney," she called after me in a mock-BBC tone, then added, more familiarly, "Poor Holly's up there, even as we speak. Dare say her ladyship's got her polishing the brass as well as slaving away in the kitchen. Bloomin' cheek, if you ask me." She jerked a thumb in the direction of the stairs. "Particularly as it leaves me with *him*."

I knew who she meant.

17

I set out for Paxham Manor that evening riddled with apprehension. I anticipated a formal occasion and had felt obliged to buy a sober-looking tie to go with my almost-white shirt.

The Manor stood a little way beyond the village, gazing down upon it from the lower slopes. Behind it, the ground rose steeply through a screen of trees, ending at the coastal path at the top of the cliffs.

Crossing the road which led out of Paxham, I passed between rusted gates and walked down a long, gravelled drive lined on either side by overgrown laurels. The house reared up in front of me, its stonework grimy, the high sash windows thirsty for paint, and the tall, stately chimneys forever blackened with the soot of decades.

My timorous knock sounded hollow on the thick oak door, eventually answered by Edward Hambling. His nervous smile probably mirrored mine and set me a little more at ease. Edward's dinner jacket and bow tie had seen better days, and I wondered if they'd been hand-me-downs from his grandfather.

"Good evening, -er, Aidan." Edward's greeting was a long way from enthusiastic, but much as I'd expected. His gaze seemed to search my face, as if he wanted to ask a question but couldn't summon up the courage.

"Good evening, Edward," I replied, as he pulled back the door to admit me.

"Do come through and meet Gran," he said.

It sounded like a threat, because meeting Gran had been the reason for my apprehension. Edward led me into a cavernous hallway, to one side of which stood a wide, wooden staircase, its panelling punctuated with gloomy oil paintings of indistinguishable Bayldon ancestors. The flagged floor was pitted and uneven, and the atmosphere funereal.

The dining room was little better: the same oak panelling, the furniture cumbersome and ancient. Ruth Bayldon occupied a chair by the sideboard, which bore a variety of hot- plates. She arose languidly as we entered. In a faded blue dress and string of pearls, she looked as haughty and uncompromising as when I'd met her the previous evening. I knew for a fact that I hadn't been invited for the pleasure of my company. Hopefully, the reason would be revealed before the evening had advanced too far.

Mrs Bayldon offered a hand, which I took, and which, in the next instant, was withdrawn: a fleeting touch, a whiff of graciousness.

"Ah, Mr Verney, and nicely punctual. Do join Edward and I in a sherry, while your friend Miss Tasker finishes off in the kitchen."

She stood aside to indicate a small silver tray, which bore three schooners of an anaemic-looking liquid. Edward stepped forward to do the honours, dutifully serving his grandmother first. She raised her glass and sipped from it primly. Believing it safe to do likewise, I followed suit, relieved that I'd taken the merest taste. The bottle boasted a label which suggested that it contained *amontillado*. I didn't feel like giving it the benefit of the doubt.

Edward stood devotedly at his grandmother's side, his awkward expression more a grimace than a grin. The faint odour of mothballs circulated from his dinner jacket. I grimaced back and dipped bravely into my sherry, wondering how to strike up a conversation. I was saved the bother, when the double doors creaked open to reveal sight of Holly's flushed but stoically smiling face.

"All ready to dish up, Mrs Bayldon."

"Thank you," Ruth replied stiffly, wincing at the girl's lack of finesse. She indicated a place at the table for me, as Holly promptly disappeared again. She sat down at the head of the table with Edward to her right, which meant that he and I faced one another across it. As we waited for Holly to bring the dishes through from the kitchen, my gaze was drawn to a portrait hung above the sideboard behind Edward's chair: the head and shoulders of a distinguished and not unkindly-looking man in an army uniform which bore the inevitable array of medals.

Ruth Bayldon swept in quickly. "A portrait of my late husband, Mr Verney. Dear Roderick. Sadly, he passed on two years ago."

"I'm sorry to hear that, Mrs Bayldon. I've -er, heard good things about him."

I wouldn't have thought it possible, but she positively glowed at the compliment, while Edward's complacent nod suggested I'd said the right thing.

74

"Thank you, Mr Verney. You're most kind. Indeed, Roderick was a good man. So public-spirited."

Holly entered, bashing through the heavy doors to the effect that Mrs Bayldon frowned, and I leapt up to lend a hand. As she brought round the dishes, I got the feeling that she was rather subdued. I returned the pale smile she gave me, as she served us in silence. I noticed that she wore a cotton skirt which almost brushed the floor: a riposte to Ruth's criticism of her 'inappropriate' attire the previous evening.

As Holly progressed round the table, I noticed Edward slavishly tracking her movements. As the girl finished serving and took a seat a little way down the table from me, Ruth Bayldon cleared her throat. I looked up, thinking she was about to speak, and caught the fearsome glare she directed at Edward, whose errant gaze immediately dropped to his plate.

The meal was frugal, although Holly had done her best with some average ingredients. She'd chopped the beef into small chunks and cooked it in a casserole, adding a variety of vegetables to make it go further. Each of us was rationed to two potatoes, and the wine, served in a carafe to disguise its supermarket provenance, might have done better in the casserole.

Conversation was kept to a minimum. I complimented Holly on her efforts and was backed up by Edward's cautious approbation, but she merely answered with a pale smile. I was surprised that, as the hired help, she'd been allowed to eat with us and believed she felt out of place. Also, she seemed to have difficulty meeting my gaze, and I wondered why that might be. Ruth Bayldon made one or two social comments, regarding her husband's work both in the community and as a Justice of the Peace. She spoke exclusively to me, ignoring the others.

Edward contributed by mentioning his paternal grandfather, the much-decorated General Marcus Hambling, whose photograph was partly obscured behind a dish of tired-looking fruit on the sideboard.

"They were both fine men," Ruth Bayldon cut in crisply. "The general remained in the military up to a great age but, having served gallantly in the last war, dear Roderick decided to channel his efforts into the betterment of the local community. In which, I believe, he greatly succeeded."

I concurred politely in the right places. In their different ways, Edward and his grandmother had been trying to impress me with an idea of the Bayldon/Hambling superiority over we lesser mortals. It made me think of my own grandfather: a millworker from aged fourteen, now hale, hearty and robustly chapel-going in his late eighties. The type of man who could be described as the salt of the earth and ranked proudly alongside any of Edward's forebears.

With almost palpable relief, we moved on to Eleanor's apple pie, where I knew we'd be on safer ground. Even Edward came out of his shell. "Sadly, General Hambling's in a nursing home," he said. "I try to visit as often as I can. But he's very old and not at all in a good way."

"I keep asking Edward if I can go with him one day," Holly chipped in, her first words for a while. "It's down at Eastbourne, isn't it? I went there once as a child, and I'd love to go again."

"The general doesn't react well to visitors," Ruth cut in icily. "But he's used to Edward, so I'd rather he went alone." She glanced around at our empty plates. "I think, Miss Tasker, that you might start clearing away."

Holly leapt up obediently, alert to the note of command. As she collected up the crockery, the phone in the hallway rang stridently.

"Perhaps you'd answer that first?" Ruth Bayldon said. It was hardly a question.

I sensed the tension in Holly, as she abandoned the plates and left the room. She returned in a matter of seconds.

"It's for you, Mrs Bayldon. A Mrs Maltravers?"

"Ah, the Mothers' Union secretary. She'll be calling for my advice." She dumped her napkin on the table, pushed past Holly and disappeared into the hallway.

Holly shot me a tight-lipped glance and resumed where she'd left off.

"Can I lend a hand?" I asked. Edward didn't seem about to offer, and I thought it all a thankless imposition on the girl.

Edward raised a timid hand, and a look of complicity seemed to pass between him and Holly. "Er – no." His voice wasn't much above a whisper. "I'd -er, like your opinion on a certain matter."

Surreptitiously, he withdrew something from his trouser pocket and passed it across the table. I saw that it was a business card, bearing an address in Walworth and the legend 'Delverton Enterprises Inc.'

Edward kept his voice low. Holly shuttled to and from the kitchen, while in the hallway Ruth Bayldon issued orders down the line in an overbearing tone. "No, Ethel. Most certainly not. The vicar must do that, and I shall tell him so. No, no, leave the matter with me and be assured that I shall attend to it."

"That man Delverton approached me in the High Street earlier today," Edward said. "There's a field behind the Manor, which actually belongs to me. He's looking to set up a caravan park, and I'm meeting up with him to talk about it. I'd like your opinion on whether I can trust -."

He broke off guiltily, as his grandmother barged back into the room, spearing him with a basilisk stare. Her telephone conversation notwithstanding, she'd obviously overheard enough. Meanwhile, I took the opportunity to scoop Delverton's card off the table and drop it unseen into my trouser pocket.

"Edward," his grandmother declared roundly, "I do hope you're not discussing that awful man who walks around Paxham as if he owns it? You're to have nothing to do with him, do you hear? We don't do business with his class of person, and in any case none of the Manor's land will be sold off in my lifetime. I totally forbid it. Now I'd be obliged if you'd remain in here, while I have a few words with Mr Verney."

Holly had come back into the room as Ruth Bayldon had been speaking. She bent her head to her work, seemingly intent on giving me a wide berth. I got to my feet, as Edward looked at me helplessly and then away.

I was on my own.

18

Whatever was about to happen was what I'd been dreading: the real reason for my invitation to the Manor that evening.

Ruth Bayldon wanted a conversation in private, but I doubted if the others would try to eavesdrop. Holly was busy in the kitchen, as evidenced by the clatter of crockery and splash of water, while Edward wouldn't dare stir from the dining room, where he'd been told to remain.

I followed her across the hallway to a slightly damp-smelling, feebly lit drawing room. Ruth swished the velvet drapes across the windows and invited me to sit. I sank obediently into the nearest armchair. A spring twanged lugubriously, and the cushion subsided to an alarming extent, making me wonder if I'd ever be able to extricate myself.

My hostess chose a wooden chair, on which she parked herself primly, hands folded in her lap. As she gazed down on me, I was reminded of a hawk circling above its prey. Without preamble, she asked what had brought me to Paxham?

The question needled me, for it wasn't asked in a conversational way, but I managed to keep my voice level. "I'm here on holiday," I replied. "I've been ill and haven't long come out of hospital."

"Then I wish you a speedy convalescence." She wasn't intending to dwell on the subject, not even bothering to inquire about the nature of my illness.

Bolt upright on her chair, Ruth Bayldon looked austere and supremely in command. "Miss Tasker has told me of your interest in the *Leesbourne Belle* tragedy, and I observed you deep in conversation this morning with that gossiping brother of Miss Neale. He's almost as bad as she is, but it is, after all, a family trait."

I was now well aware of the reason for this interrogation and determined to hold my ground. If I were to buckle, I was sure she'd have me on the next train out of Paxham, even going so far as to frogmarch me down to the station herself. I tried to inject some self-belief into my reply, bolstering it with a white lie.

"I'm a bit of a local history student, Mrs Bayldon, and take a passing interest in the history of the places I visit. My interest in the ferry sinking was sparked by a conversation with Miss Instow. She happened to have known Georgie Kell, one of the victims."

"Miss Instow's memory isn't likely to be served by your 'passing interest' in a twenty-one-year-old tragedy," she hit back scornfully. "I met Miss Instow – she took tea with me here. I'm sorry about what happened to her, but she herself admitted she might have been confused. She'd dealt with so many small children in her capacity as a district nurse, that she might well have mistaken Georgie for another boy."

Privately, I dismissed that statement out of hand but, as Ruth was talking, I suddenly remembered that it had been *Edward* with whom Connie Instow had wished to speak. I realised that she'd never actually done so and boldly put the matter to my hostess.

"Yes, she did say she wanted to meet him, but sadly she never got the chance." Ruth pointed to a framed photograph above the fireplace of an attractive, smiling, dark-haired girl in a crisp white dress. "Madeleine was very dear to us." I didn't imagine the catch in her voice. "Even now, I feel the pain of her loss, something with which my dear late husband never came to terms."

Snowy Neale's words came back to me. *"It won't ever go away."* And I felt chastened. I could imagine how her grief had festered and how it would always be present.

"I'm sorry, Mrs Bayldon," I apologised. "As I've said, my only motive was a passing interest, and I certainly wouldn't wish to cause you any further distress."

"Well, so long as you understand that." Her expression lapsed into a wintry smile. "I take it you'll shortly be returning home? Where might that be?"

I named the little Oxfordshire town where I lived. "I'm here for two more days."

"Then I hope you enjoy the rest of your stay and have a safe journey home."

She already seemed to be waving me off from the station. But I was beyond irritation now, for escape was in sight. I thanked her for that evening's invitation.

"My pleasure." Her tone was one of strained graciousness.

I had no other option but to stand, for I'd been dismissed. She escorted me out to the hallway. There was no sign of Holly or Edward, but I felt sure they were skulking close by. I tugged open the door, stepped outside and wished Mrs Bayldon good evening. She'd closed the door on me, almost before the reply had left her lips.

I walked away from the Manor and its faded grandeur; from its mistress and her crippling grief over the loss of a dearly loved daughter; from the way she clung grimly to past glories in the vain hope of recreating days long gone. I recognised her deep, desperate sadness and pitied her for it.

It was after ten when I got back to Harbour Heights. Eleanor Neale was waiting in reception, sitting in a corner with some knitting, the area lit by the weak glow of a table lamp.

"Sorry," I said. "Am I the last?"

"Huh!" Her tone was disparaging. "Not closing time yet, is it? The ladies are in bed, though." She made a point of peering behind me, adding tartly, "I thought Holly might have come back with you?"

"Er, she was finishing clearing away. I don't think she'll be long."

Eleanor placed her knitting on the desk. "I'd better set about making some cocoa, then."

We took it through to the lounge, settling near the door to intercept the latecomers. Eleanor's sharp ears soon caught a movement. "That you, Holly?"

A head peeped tentatively round the corner. Holly looked slightly guilty, and I guessed that she'd hoped to slip quietly upstairs.

"Oh, um – hi, Miss Neale and -um, Mr Verney."

"Formal all of a sudden, aren't we? Come and sit in here, while I fetch you a mug of cocoa."

Eleanor bustled away, and Holly came in, looking uncertain. She sat down beside me, close enough for me to detect, above her perfume, the odours of that evening's toil in the Manor's kitchen.

She turned to me anxiously, once more having difficulty looking me in the face. "Aidan, I owe you an apology. Mrs Bayldon learned about your interest in the ferry from me. I didn't mean to drop you in it, but somehow, she wormed it out of me. The only reason she invited you there was to give you a ticking off. Oh, and that dinner was *awful.* I was ashamed of it."

"You did the best you could. And it doesn't matter about Mrs Bayldon. She scares me too."

Her hand rested on the arm of her chair and, summoning up my courage, I gently placed mine over it, before insinuating it into hers. At that moment, Eleanor materialised in the doorway, and our hands quickly parted. Eleanor gave a good impression of not having noticed, but her small, informed smile assured me she had.

She handed Holly her mug, and the girl thanked her and stood up. I forestalled her.

"Holly, before you go. You too, Miss Neale. About Mr Delverton? Do you think you'd be inclined to trust him?"

Holly looked doubtful, but Eleanor's response was instantaneous. "Not with my grandmother's false teeth. His type's always up to something. Why do you ask?"

"It's just that this evening, Edward started to ask my advice – something to do with Delverton approaching him?"

Holly was nodding. "He tried asking me too," she said. "But his gran interrupted."

"Same here."

"Funny, though," Holly went on. "Edward usually keeps me at arm's length, but tonight, soon after I got there, he came into the kitchen, looking very worried. It must be about money. He teaches piano, you see, but we're already into the Autumn term, and he's only got two pupils. He'd hoped to make a profit from last night's concert but barely broke even."

"He stands to inherit from General Hambling, doesn't he?" I put in.

"Oh, he's the sole heir, which explains why he's so dutiful. Granny B makes sure he pays regular visits. The general's old and very ill, but he could go on for ages."

"What did he manage to say to you about Delverton?" I asked. "He started to tell me about him wanting to buy some land."

"He didn't get that far before his gran interrupted us and sent him packing."

"Some land was settled on Edward's mother by her grandparents," Eleanor said. "So, it actually belongs to him. He's over twenty-one, so by rights, he could sell if he wished."

Holly and I shook our heads simultaneously. "He won't dare," I said. "Mrs Bayldon came in and told him in no uncertain terms that he's not selling. I have a feeling Delverton's idea for a caravan park won't get far."

"*A caravan park?*" Eleanor screeched. "Her ladyship wouldn't allow that, even if the Manor fell down around her ears. Which won't be long, the way things are going."

Our conversation was halted as the outer door slammed, followed by the sound of a stifled belch. Eleanor whisked out into reception, greeted Delverton and handed him his room key, for which he burbled his thanks before blundering away up the stairs.

As Eleanor re-joined us, I wondered aloud if there might have been a connection between Delverton and Connie Instow?

Her interest was immediately fired. "Funny you should say that, Mr Verney. Miss Instow never said as much, but I got the impression she recognised him from somewhere. And he seemed a bit furtive around her. Mind you, his type's always furtive."

I went up to my room with much to think about. But to my surprise, tiredness soon overtook me, and I slept soundly.

19

On awakening, my mind was an instant jumble of suppositions. I reflected ironically that I was no longer moping over the loss of Diana.

I got ready and went down to breakfast. Eleanor was her usual brisk self and the ladies bright and chatty, although Holly seemed a little out of sorts. Tony Delverton had yet to put in an appearance, so it couldn't be blamed on him.

However, as she brought me breakfast, she did ask what were my plans for the day.

"A long walk, for certain," I replied.

She forced a smile. "You'll need plenty of fresh air to clear away the memory of that awful dinner."

"Goodness me, was it that bad?" Eleanor had been hovering nearby.

"She did very well," I said gallantly, rewarded by her look of gratitude.

"I'll make you up some sandwiches for lunchtime, Mr Verney," Eleanor offered. She directed a nod at Holly. "This one surprised me this morning. Must have been up at the crack of dawn. She was making her way up from the harbour, as I was fetching the milk in. Don't know what's come over her. Usually has to be shaken awake."

"I couldn't sleep," Holly protested. "Must've been all those hours I spent in the Manor's grotty old kitchen." She twitched a smile at me. "I needed a walk to clear my head, too."

Eleanor moved on, and Holly went to fetch the ladies a fresh pot of tea, leaving me puzzled. She'd seemed jumpy when Eleanor had made her comment, and I wondered why.

Eleanor handed me my sandwiches as I was about to leave and wished me a relaxing day with my sketching. But as I set off, I knew I wouldn't be doing much in the way of that; neither would the day be relaxing.

I was worried and confused. Since finding her on that ledge, I'd often wondered if Connie Instow's death might not have been an accident. From then on, certain things had happened, certain information had come my way, and the conclusion I felt bound to draw from it all horrified me.

I needed time to get my thoughts in order, so I walked down to the harbour and out along the estuary. The colourful scenery, and the sunlight which made a mirror of the sea, meant nothing to me. People walked past, but I didn't really notice them, replying with a distracted grunt or nod to several cheery 'Good mornings.'

Eventually needing a rest, I sat on a boulder overlooking the Channel and used my sketch pad to make a list of my thoughts. The longer the list grew, the more I felt troubled by it.

Annie Midson was key to my thoughts. At Colonel Bayldon's insistence, she'd not gone to the chapel of rest for a last look at Georgie's body. Indeed, she'd had to remain in hospital herself for a while.

Neither, as far as I could ascertain, did Annie set eyes on Edward Hambling. He was tutored at home for more than a year, before being packed off to boarding school; gone by the time Annie was offered work at the Manor. And neither his nurse nor tutor had been Paxham residents who'd known the boy previously.

The Bayldons had been kind to Annie, helping her financially even though far from well off themselves. Might there have been truth in the rumour of a relationship between Annie and the colonel?

Annie Midson had turned to drink. Had she fallen down the stairs while under the influence, or were there more sinister implications? It had been Colonel Bayldon who'd found her.

And I'd been warned off by Ruth Bayldon the previous night.

My thoughts turned to Madeleine Hambling. There was no question over her bravery. She'd stayed in the water, risking her life to rescue Georgie Kell. Yet several people had remarked to me that you 'couldn't tell the boys apart'; and Snowy had said they were 'as like as two peas in a pod'; and that on the day of the tragedy, they were wearing similar outfits.

What if Madeleine had remained in the water *in an unsuccessful bid to rescue her own son?*

Then I moved on to Connie Instow. She'd never got to meet Edward but had known Georgie Kell as a toddler. If she'd met Edward, *might she have recognised him as Georgie?*

Had that been the Bayldons' dilemma? Edward was General Hambling's sole heir, for the general's two sons and daughter-in-law were dead. If it were proved or even suspected that the real Edward Hambling had perished in the ferry sinking, the Bayldon's grandson (and by implication his grandmother) wouldn't inherit the general's money: money which could save Paxham Manor from falling into ruin.

Rumours, Eleanor Neale had said. *There'd always been rumours.* Was there perhaps some truth in them after all?

*

I'd taken the long, semi-circular walk behind Paxham that morning, although, in my preoccupation, my footsteps had led me. Having noted down my thoughts and concerns, I looked around and discovered that I'd emerged on to the coastal path between Paxham and the next village down the coast. From where I sat, I had a glimpse of St Audric's chapel on the cliffs a mile or so back towards Paxham. I was beginning to feel hungry and, with Eleanor's sandwiches and a water bottle in my rucksack, decided to head for the ruins and eat lunch there, while idly watching the ferries crossing the channel from Weymouth.

St Audric's chapel, reputed to date from the eleventh century and named in honour of a priest martyred during the Norman invasion, consisted of three-and-a-half grey stone walls providing sufficient shade to make me comfortable enough to lie down and nod off. I awoke with a start, disturbed by a noise which sounded nearby.

Listening carefully, I made out a man's voice, mumbling. I couldn't distinguish the words but guessed it was one person, talking alone. The mumbling ended in a deep sigh, tortured and forlorn.

I left my things and crept to the corner of the wall. On a rock not five yards away sat Edward Hambling, his shoulders hunched and head in hands. I didn't wish to intrude and decided it'd be best to leave him there but, as I hesitated, Edward suddenly looked round, startled to find that he wasn't alone.

"Hello, Edward." I got to my feet and appeared in full view, wearing what I hoped was a reassuring smile. "Everything all right?"

"Oh. Er, hello." Edward's scowl showed that he was distracted and my interruption unwelcome. "What brings you here?"

I explained that I'd been out for a long walk along the estuary and round the back of Paxham to join the coastal path not far beyond the ruined chapel. I enthused over the beautiful scenery.

"Yes, isn't it?" Edward was unimpressed.

"I stopped off here for a bite to eat." I went back and retrieved the sandwiches from my rucksack, now sweating slightly in their paper bag. "Miss Neale's finest: cheese and pickle. Like one?"

"No, thanks."

"Do you mind if I do?"

A grunt signified his permission.

I went and perched on a rock a few feet away from him. I unwrapped the sandwiches and took a bite, aware that he was staring vacantly out to sea.

"Everything's not all right, is it, Edward?" I suggested gently.

He flicked me a wary glance. He looked anxious, torn; seemed to be weighing up his options as to whether or not he might safely confide in me. Finally, he said, "No. No, it isn't."

I held his glance. "If you want to talk, I'm happy to listen."

Edward stared back at me for several moments. I could almost hear the question whirring in his brain: *can I trust him?* I didn't think that Edward, a self-contained young man, incarcerated with his music and hampered by his class, had anyone by way of a friend, someone with whom he might share confidences. Clearly, Holly had tried to befriend him, but he'd kept her at bay, no doubt encouraged by his grandmother.

Edward got to his feet, snatched his gaze away and went back to looking out to sea. I wondered if the moment had passed, but then he turned and faced me.

"I love it here," he said. "This spot's always been my private place. Only walkers ever come here, stop a while, read the information board and look round the ruins. They soon pass on, and I'm left here, just me alone. I used to come here in the hols, any time when I've needed solitude. I often bring some manuscript paper and do some composing. I hate the Manor – always have. It's like a mausoleum."

I decided it was time for plain speaking. He was either going to welcome it or take umbrage. "Why do you hate it?" I asked. "Does your gran cramp your style?"

His stiff expression collapsed into a guilty grin. "Yes, I suppose she does. The Manor's crumbling around us, and I just can't get her to see sense. Grandad Hambling could go on for *years*."

"But she won't hear of you selling the field?"

"That's just it!" Edward's exclamation was close to a shout. "She's completely dug in her heels. I mean, I don't like Delverton either. But we desperately need the money. And it's a useless old field that we occasionally rent out for grazing."

"Is Delverton offering a reasonable price?" I asked.

"Any price is a good price," Edward groaned.

"What I mean is, is he offering the proper value?" I persisted. "And more to the point, do you trust him?"

"I've been to see the family solicitor," he replied doggedly. "The field's mine to dispose of, although Gran's advised me not to be hasty."

Footsteps sounded on the gravel track, and we both looked round. I didn't think the conversation would have got much further. Mrs Bayldon had strongly advised against selling; and her word seemed to be law.

Holly appeared round the chapel wall, casual in jeans, T-shirt and trainers. "Oh, there you are, Edward. I wondered if I might find you up here. Nelly said I could have the afternoon off, although I must be back by five. Hi, Aidan." I was gratified to see her expression brighten. "What brings you here?"

"My long walk," I replied. "I stopped here for lunch and met Edward. Can I offer you a sandwich?"

"Oh, please. I'm famished." She took one and bit into it energetically, before turning to Edward. "Are you up here writing one of your symphonies?" she asked.

The question was asked in good faith, but Edward quickly put her down. "I don't compose *symphonies*." He'd withdrawn into himself, his tone dismissive. "So, no – I'm not."

"Oh, poor you. You should try not to let Gran upset you so much."

"She's not your gran," he said coldly. Looking sullen, he turned away. "I'm sorry. There are things on my mind, and I'm poor company." He stole a glance at his watch. "In fact, I need to be somewhere else."

"You're not by any chance meeting Delverton?" I asked, sensing Holly's keen stare.

He didn't look at me, but I could tell from the instant flush on his cheeks that I'd guessed right. "A new pupil," he said. "I'm meeting his father."

Looking at Holly, I could tell we were on the same wavelength: Edward was a poor liar.

I plunged in, because the question had been on my mind all morning. "Edward, does Delverton have some kind of hold over you?"

Holly gasped, staring at me open-mouthed. But Edward was furious.

"Now you're being ridiculous!" he snapped. "What's the matter with you? First you upset Gran with your stupid questions about the *Leesbourne Belle*, and now you're trying to get at me!"

Holly had quickly recovered, and her expression was one of pity.

"No, he's not, Edward. He's simply trying to help you."

She reached out towards him, but he dashed her hand away, his features pinched, and mouth twisted in spite. "I don't want his help, or yours, or anyone's. Why don't you both go away and just *leave me alone!*"

The last words leapt out in a shriek, and Edward scrambled over the rocks and stormed off in the direction of Paxham.

Holly, looking distressed, made to follow, but I held her back by the arm. "Let him go," I said.

"But Aidan, do you really think Delverton's trying to *cheat* him?"

She seemed on the verge of tears, and I wondered why she should be taking it so much to heart.

"I don't know," I replied candidly. "All I have are suspicions. But I think, for Edward's sake, we should try to find out. If he is about to meet up with Delverton, there are no prizes for guessing where that'll be."

20

We set off in pursuit. Edward was moving at pace, head down and hands thrust deep in trouser pockets. He took loping strides, fuelled by his unhappiness, and soon outdistanced us. I felt sure I knew where he was heading and that we didn't need to keep up with him. It'd be best not to anyway, in case he looked round and spotted us. But he seemed too securely wrapped in his own misery to notice us.

Once we'd reached Paxham, I suggested we walked along above the quay to circle round behind the Lobster Pot, so that Edward wouldn't catch sight of us straight away. I wanted to get a flavour of the conversation, although I had a good idea what it'd be about.

It was the middle of the lunch period, and the pub was busy, the babble of voices, pipe smoke and beer fumes billowing out from the open windows and doorway. As we stole down the far side of the pub, I spotted Tony Delverton, lounging at one of the picnic benches on the quay, a pint glass at his elbow. There were people at most of the other tables, although Delverton was seated slightly apart from any of them.

Edward stood beside him with his back to us, awkward and out of place. He was speaking, his voice low and urgent in his desperation. I took Holly by the arm and held her back, so that we remained out of sight but well within earshot.

Edward had finished saying his piece. He shifted his stance, and I saw his anguish. His head was lolling, face pale, and his arms hung limply by his sides, like a discarded rag doll.

Taking a leisurely swig of beer, Delverton eyed him mysteriously from behind his shades. The jocular tone couldn't mask his coldness.

"You're going to have to try a bit harder to get your gran to see sense, Eddie. This gossipy lot love a juicy rumour. Trouble is, rumours have a habit of spreading: maybe even all the way along to Eastbourne.

"So, here's what I recommend. Pop down and have a chat with the general. I'm sure he'd let you have a couple of hundred, if you ask him nicely. That'll be enough to keep me sweet, until you can persuade your gran to let me have that field at a decent price. You run along and give it some thought, now. I'll be around for a few days more. But I can't wait forever."

"What you said just now?" Edward's words were slurred, almost as if he was drunk. "Look – it's not true, you know. Gran would say -."

Delverton bared his teeth in a mocking grin. "Yeah, what *would* she say? You wouldn't know anything about it, sunshine. You were too young to remember. And listen, it'd be best if you didn't force me to go down that route, 'cause you might hear something which'd upset you even more."

He'd not spoken in a loud voice, but its low, even timbre made it sound more menacing. I decided I couldn't listen any longer. Edward cut a dejected figure, and I pitied him. I took Holly's hand, and we emerged from the shadow of the pub. I sensed a reluctance about her, that she didn't want a confrontation.

"So, how are things going, Edward?" I inquired, as we pulled up a little way from where they stood.

89

Edward turned, his mouth agape. He looked defeated, his words trickling out. "A-Aidan. Holly. You followed me. Why?"

Delverton cut across him, clearly angry. "Here, what *is* all this? This is a private business discussion. We don't want you here. Either of you."

People at the other tables had become aware of the disturbance and sat looking on. I'd always shunned being the centre of attention but felt the occasion demanded it.

"Doesn't sound much like a business discussion to me," I replied evenly. "I thought I heard you asking Edward for money, but as I understood it, *you* were supposed to be buying from *him.*"

Delverton swung his legs over the bench and stood up. He'd whipped off his shades to reveal eyes sparking with hatred, while his perfect white smile had somersaulted into a snarl.

He jabbed a finger in my face, blasting me with beery breath. "Like I said, pal, you're not wanted." The finger moved towards Holly. "As for you, sweetheart, you ought to keep well out of it, if you know what's good for you."

Her hand trembled in my grasp, and she cowered behind me, while Edward looked on, dumbfounded.

Delverton started to turn away. I reached out a hand to stop him, and he stared at it with contempt.

"Just a word, Mr Delverton." I kept my voice low, so that only the three of them might hear me. "Why don't you leave Paxham now? Because what you were suggesting to Edward sounded very much like blackmail, and the police would take a dim view of it."

Delverton dashed the hand away. "Get lost." He turned to Edward. "Just think it over, Eddie. You know where to find me."

It happened quickly. Delverton had turned on his heel to walk away, certainly not needing the attention he was getting. Holly came out of hiding and moved forward to console Edward. I was close behind her and froze in astonishment, for Edward's face was crimson, he was quivering with rage, and his fists were bunched. He shoved Holly aside, and she staggered back into me. Then, with a bellow of rage from deep in his being, he flung himself at Delverton, before I was able to react.

Delverton turned too late, as Edward slammed into him, his hands reaching for the throat. They crashed back against a table, from behind which a couple leapt to their feet in alarm. Glasses flew off and shattered on the ground. The noise of the fracas quickly reached the pub, and people spilled out to discover the cause of it.

Delverton struggled to defend himself, but Edward's hands were at his throat, the tapered fingers digging into the flesh. All his frustration had erupted in a frenzy: the failed recital, lack of money, the vicious rumours.

I snapped out of my stupor, moved Holly aside, charged in and tried to pull Edward away. I couldn't budge him. Out of the corner of my eye, I saw Irene Pake burst through the gaggle of spectators. She looked furious. Snowy Neale was behind her and tugged her back, before wading in to help me.

Together, we managed to separate them, but even as we restrained him, Edward fought to get at Delverton, who looked shocked and speechless as he massaged his injured throat.

"I'll *kill* you, if you don't leave me alone, Delverton," Edward stormed. "Do you hear me? I promise I'll *kill* you!"

Irene marched up and told Delverton in no uncertain terms to leave and not show his face near the Lobster Pot again. She stood over him, arms akimbo, while he stared back, hot eyes cursing her. Finally, he turned and slunk off without a word.

Bet Parrish came forward and took charge of Holly. "You look peaky, lovey. Come and sit over here." She guided her to the nearest table and sat beside her, an arm around her shoulders. The girl was close to tears, unable to look at any of us.

"Better sit him down, too, Aidan." Bet nodded at Edward, who stood beside me, bemused and shivering. "Okay if I get him a brandy, Irene?" she asked.

Irene's expression was thunderous. "As long as he pays for it," she snarled. "One thing I won't have here is brawling. My dad never allowed it, and nor do I." The lecture was directed at Edward, but I doubted that he was capable of taking it in.

Snowy offered to sort out the brandy, and Irene stalked back into the pub to reappear with a dustpan and broom. She swept up the debris and had mellowed sufficiently to replace any drinks that had been spilled.

I sat Edward down opposite Bet and Holly. He glared at us all. "Can't any of you *see*?" he burst out, plunging a finger in the direction of Delverton, now a hundred yards or more along the quay. "That man! He could *ruin* me!"

21

"Edward, what do you mean? Ruin you?" Holly asked anxiously.

He refused to look at her and, seeing she was upset, Bet hugged her closer.

Most of the crowd had dispersed, going back into the pub. Irene, having cleared up the mess, went after them. A few people remained, talking in low voices and flicking the occasional glance in Edward's direction. Snowy Neale, returning with the brandy, noticed this, set the glass down in front of Edward and moved round to stand behind the two women, his massive frame blocking the onlookers' view.

"It's the things he's saying," Edward groaned, staring down at his feet and addressing no-one in particular. "He – he says he knows something about – about my past."

"I wouldn't give him the time of day," Bet declared. "He's spreading silly rumours that no-one in their right mind would believe." She waved a dismissive hand in the direction Delverton had gone. "I really hope this means we've seen the last of him."

Snowy rested a supportive hand on her shoulder. "I know, pet. He's too familiar by half. But Irene meant what she said: there's no way she'll have him back in the Lobster."

Bet smiled up at him and patted his hand. Holly, too, seemed to take heart from Snowy's words. She turned to Edward.

"Delverton's a cheat and a liar," she said. "He's hard up and out to make a quick buck. I shall tell Miss Neale what's happened, and it wouldn't surprise me if she kicks him out of the hotel."

Bet gave her a squeeze. "And not a moment too soon in my opinion."

"Ah, our Nell won't hold wi' no nonsense," Snowy put in.

Holly got to her feet and walked over to Edward. "Come back to the hotel with Aidan and me. I'll make some tea to calm us all down."

But Edward shook his head, still wouldn't make eye contact. "No," he answered sullenly. "I'd rather be alone." He switched me a savage glance. "I'm sure you'll be fine without me." He got up, turned his back on us all and hurried off along the quay, leaving the brandy untouched.

"Whew!" Bet exclaimed, once he was out of earshot. "He's in a strop. Good job you and Snowy were around, Aidan, else we might have had a murder on our hands."

"Probably would have, if Irene had got her mitts on Delverton," Snowy chuckled.

"Hey!"

We all whirled round. Irene stood in the pub doorway, looking annoyed. "You staying out there all day, Bet? There are customers in here want serving."

Bet raised a weary eyebrow. "No rest for the wicked." She hauled herself to her feet and went back inside with Snowy.

I sat down beside Holly. Everyone else had gone.

"I wish I knew what was going on," she sighed. "Do *you* know, Aidan?"

I indicated the chapel at the far end of the harbour. "Let's go there. It'll be quiet, and we can talk."

We got up and started walking. I slipped a stealthy hand into hers and was glad that she didn't pull away.

"The trouble is," I went on, "I don't actually *know* anything. There's nothing I can prove. But you've a right to hear it, although I don't think you'll like it." As she turned towards me, looking apprehensive, I added, "I don't like it either and I really hope I'm wrong."

It was cool in the chapel and, as I'd hoped, deserted. I lit a candle, placed it on the rack and stood in silence over it for a few moments, before returning to where she was sitting.

She'd been watching me and looked puzzled. "Why did you do that?" she asked.

"It's for remembrance," I said. "I was saying a prayer for Connie."

"For Miss Instow?" She took hold of my arm. "That's a lovely thought, Aidan. You liked her, didn't you?"

"It was difficult not to like her, and I only wish there'd been more time to get to know her. She didn't deserve to die like that."

"But it was just an unfortunate accident," Holly protested. And when I didn't reply, she added uncertainly, "Wasn't it?"

"I'm not sure. But I don't think it was."

"You don't? Then -?"

I placed a finger to my lips, and she fell silent. She sat beside me, tense, her hand dropping to her side, her gaze not leaving my face. I felt for her, because I couldn't be sure how she'd take this.

I reached down to my rucksack and brought out my sketchpad. I turned to the notes I'd made that morning and glanced quickly through them. They seemed more poignant after the altercation outside the Lobster Pot; and also seemed to confirm my suspicion that Delverton was involved somewhere.

I wondered if Holly might peer over my shoulder at what I'd written, but her whole attention remained fixed on me. Her mouth hung slightly open, and there was something in her eyes which I couldn't define. I wondered later if it might have been fear.

I tried to let her down as gently as I could, but even so, she was appalled at what I had to say.

The man we know as Edward might really be Georgie Kell? *Surely,* that can't be true?"

"I hope not, I really do. Nothing can be proved. There are no hard facts, only suppositions. But if it were true, do you think Mrs Bayldon would ever admit it?"

Holly grimaced. "Not in a million years."

"The real problem lies with Delverton," I went on. "How's he managed to get hold of this? I can't believe he's just come here and seized on a rumour. Who's been feeding him this information?"

94

Holly was confused and upset. "I need time to get my head round this," she groaned. "It's *awful*."

She looked up imploringly, and her hand found mine. "You're worried about Edward, aren't you?" I prompted her.

She nodded. "Yes, I am. He's been really odd recently, so frustrated by his gran making decisions for him. And now this thing with Delverton. Aidan, he's not strong, and it's all pushing him so close to the edge. You've seen how highly strung he is. I'm worried that he might do – well, something even worse than he's done today."

"Would it help if you talked to him?"

She shook her head. "He won't listen. I keep trying, but he's not interested in me. And I'm not interested in him either, Aidan. Just that I thought he might appreciate a friend."

I believed I knew what she was trying to say, but something held her back from putting it into words. There was a plea in her eyes, but I needed to be certain what it was before I could try to answer it.

"Holly," I said. "Something's worrying you. Please, tell me what it is. I want to help."

She looked up at me: the tears had returned. She gripped my hand firmly, clung to it.

"It's Delverton, isn't it?" She didn't reply, and I followed up with the question I'd put

to Edward earlier that day. "Has he got some sort of hold over you?"

Her tears fell then. She laid her head against my chest, and I held her in my arms, waiting patiently for her to speak.

When, finally, she did, it was in a hushed whisper. "It's nothing, Aidan. It's not him – it's the type of man he is. Someone was cruel to me once, hurt me. It's just that Delverton reminds me of him."

I continued to hold her until she'd finished crying, offered my handkerchief, thankfully a clean one, so that she could dry her eyes. She looked up and smiled wanly. The plea remained.

I felt dejected, for a barrier remained between us. I'd tried but couldn't persuade her to open her heart to me, let me know what was truly troubling her. Because I wasn't convinced that what she'd just told me was the truth. I desperately wanted to help her, to offer a lifeline, because I found I was beginning to care for her, in her loneliness, in her fear.

I should have said as much to her then. But I had so little experience in such matters; and Holly had said all she was likely to say. We walked back to the hotel in silence, hand in tentative hand.

Eleanor was at the reception desk, examining a leaflet with Gibbs and Moriarty, while behind us people were passing along the street. I wished we could have been oblivious to them all, just Holly and I, so that we could each say what we needed to say.

But for now, all I could do was offer what reassurance I could. I pulled her into a corner of the porch, where we kissed. She seemed, again, to cling to me, not wanting to let me go. When our faces drew apart, I squeezed her hand, and she returned the pressure uncertainly.

She whispered that she needed to be in the kitchen and headed for it, while I made the instant decision not to go up to my room. I intended to sit with my sketchpad for a while and hope to get my thoughts in order. Neither Eleanor nor the ladies had seen me, and I was able to creep away without appearing rude.

I went up the cliff path and settled down in the shady screen of trees, which overlooked Paxham Manor. I sketched the house, trying to commit to paper its gauntness, its auras of sadness and disillusionment. I'd not been long at this before the Manor's huge front door yawned open, and Tony Delverton stepped out.

Although some distance away, I had a good view of his face. He looked smug. Ruth Bayldon appeared in the doorway, arms folded and expression bleak as she watched him leave. She withdrew and closed the door firmly.

I watched him stroll down the drive and out of sight. Later, as I made my way back to Harbour Heights, I passed the High Street pub, the Jolly Boatman, and glimpsed Delverton at the bar, flirting with the barmaid, pint glass in hand. Several people clamoured round him, as if he was the life and soul of the party.

I thought I could guess what he'd gone to see Ruth Bayldon about and wondered if she'd given in to his demands.

96

22

All was quiet in reception when I got back to the hotel that afternoon, although Eleanor, working at the desk, switched me a mysterious smile as she handed over my key. I hesitated, thinking she might be about to explain the reason, but all she said was that she hoped I'd had a good afternoon sketching and bent her head to her work.

My first thought was that she'd somehow witnessed the kiss Holly and I had shared in the porch earlier, because Eleanor Neale missed very little. But, as she wasn't about to elaborate, I went up to my room for a rest before dinner.

She was behaving oddly at dinner, too, clearly excited about something and extra-attentive to the ladies. Holly and I exchanged a puzzled glance.

Eleanor had been talking to Gibbs and Moriarty about the beautiful views down the coastline just before sunset and had cajoled them into taking a short walk after dinner and have coffee on their return.

As Holly cleared the tables, Eleanor went so far as to accompany the ladies to the doorway. I wandered into reception as she came scurrying back, having seen them on their way.

"Mr Verney – in the lounge, now! I'll fetch Holly." Eleanor's excitement had risen a notch or two, and she looked a little flushed.

I went and sat in the lounge, quickly joined by Holly, who looked bemused. Eleanor bustled in behind her and set the coffee machine in motion. Then she came over, plumped down in the armchair opposite us and grinned triumphantly.

"He's *gone!*"

Holly and I stared at one another blankly for a moment. "Sorry," I said. "Who's gone?"

"*Him.* Mr Delverton."

Holly's face suddenly seemed to clear. "You're saying Delverton's *left?*"

"Yes. This afternoon. I was in reception, and down he came, bold as you like, carrying his holdall."

"I thought I heard him out here talking," Holly said, relieved. "I stayed in the kitchen to keep well clear."

"So, has he left Paxham?" I inquired.

Eleanor shook her head. "Gone round to the Boatman. Reckoned we were overpriced here – bloomin' cheek! – and didn't feel he was welcome. Well, he got that right. He decided he hadn't that much cash on him, which was hardly surprising after all that beer he drank, so he paid me a cheque – hope to goodness it doesn't bounce. Anyway, he's out of our hair. And, of course, I didn't let on that I knew what it was all about."

She looked expectantly from one of us to the other, a cat at a mousehole. "And I believe," she went on, "that the two of you were there. A right set-to, wasn't it?"

It transpired that one of the local fishermen had mentioned it to her not long after it had happened, but Eleanor was eager for as much gory detail as she could glean. Between us, Holly and I told her what had happened outside the Lobster Pot that lunchtime.

Eleanor chuckled maliciously. "I should reckon Irene Pake's scared our Mr Delverton half to death. A real firebrand, that one, and always was. Set her cap at our Jim more than once, and then the minute she gets herself a new barmaid, he goes and falls for *her*. It'll take a long time for Irene to forgive him that. Never quite had the way with men: not that she was a bad-looking lass, but too quick to fly off the handle. Some say she was married for a while up in London, during the war. But nothing came of it, and she moved back here to take over the pub from her dad. Well, that's enough gossip for now, and that sounds like the ladies coming back. We'll relax and have our coffee, because there won't be any need for me to sit up tonight, waiting for somebody to roll in late!"

*

I awoke with a start. It had been a balmy night, and I'd slept with the window open. Several people were shouting, voices raised above the usual screech of seagulls, and the noise seemed to be carrying up from the harbour. My watch told me it was just after five o'clock.

I heard movement on the floor below, scrambled out of bed and pulled a jumper over my pyjama top. I looked out of the door, saw a light on the landing below

98

and went down. Eleanor Neale stood outside her room, swathed in a tartan dressing gown.

"Those shouts wake you up?" she asked. "They did me. Enough to wake the dead. What on earth's going on?"

"Sounds as if something's happened down at the harbour," I said.

"I should think it has!"

Farther along the landing, a door opened, and the startled faces of Gibbs and Moriarty peeped out, one with her hair in curlers, the other with a sinister silk mask pushed up over her forehead. "What's happening?" they asked simultaneously.

Eleanor cocked a challenging eye at me. "I don't know, ladies. But Mr Verney and I'll go down there and take a look. I'll wake Holly – surprised she can sleep through that row – and get her to make you a cup of tea."

I hurried back to my room, threw on some clothes and returned to the lower landing. Eleanor stood outside an open door farther along, looking puzzled.

"She's gone," she said.

"Gone? Holly?" I immediately felt uneasy. The shouting on the quay: *Holly?*

"No idea, but she's not in her room."

"Perhaps she's downstairs – in the kitchen?" I snatched at the first available straw, hoping she was, but knowing in my heart that she wouldn't be there.

Eleanor told the ladies, who'd remained in their doorway, that Holly must have gone to the harbour before us, and she'd sort out tea for everyone once we'd returned. This seemed to appease them, and they withdrew into their room.

Downstairs, we quickly checked kitchen, dining room and lounge, but found no sign of Holly. Yet, she must have gone out, because the bolt on the main door had been drawn back.

We went outside, the shouts sounding louder now, and started walking towards the harbour. I sensed a tension in Eleanor. It couldn't match what I was feeling. *Where had Holly gone?*

The sun's first rays were beginning to peep over the cliffs beyond Leesbourne, and in the dim light we could make out a small crowd at the far end of the quay. As we drew nearer, I noticed PC Curtis's Panda car at the side of the Lobster Pot, Snowy's white thatch prominent among a knot of fishermen, and the tall figure of a woman, dark hair down beyond her shoulders, who I guessed must be Irene Pake. They were drawn together around something on the quay, obscuring our view of it.

A mantra was thumping in my brain: *where was Holly? Where was she?* As we walked, picking up our pace, I peered earnestly forward, seeking a redeeming glimpse of her blonde head.

I couldn't see her there.

I began to feel slightly sick. Eleanor sensed my growing distress and took my arm. "She'll be all right, dear." Her voice was kind, trying to set my mind at rest. "Don't worry."

As we hurried on, the crowd, as if by prior arrangement, drew apart, and I saw something on the ground, covered by a tarpaulin, water pooling beneath it. Curtis's inarguable figure stood over it. Beyond him, a car had pulled up alongside his. A bespectacled man in a trilby hat got out and strode across, carrying a briefcase.

We'd reached the edge of the crowd by then. I couldn't snatch my gaze away from what lay beneath the tarpaulin. Tears welled up in my eyes, almost blinding me, my heart was racing, and I was having difficulty breathing. Eleanor gripped my arm more tightly, uttered more consoling words.

I didn't hear them; had gone beyond hearing them. How I managed to remain on my feet, I should never know. The sun's rays danced in the pale sky, the prelude to a beautiful day. Surely, what was happening in front of me couldn't be for real? Surely, it had to be part of a hideous dream, from which I'd soon awake? *Where was she? Where was she?*

Then, out of a strange silence, arose Curtis's voice, almost sepulchral, addressing the new arrival. "Fished out these last ten minutes, Doc. Pretty sure there's no hope, but you'd better check."

We watched, stricken, as the doctor crouched down and peeled back a corner of the tarpaulin. I felt my senses starting to fade...

Several gasps went up from the crowd; and then we were staring down at the pale, bloated face of Tony Delverton.

A voice spoke from behind me. "I heard the shouts and raced down here. Snowy told me to run up and fetch Bet."

It was a voice I knew...

23

I looked across and saw Bet Parrish, an overcoat round her shoulders, standing next to Irene Pake. Beside me, Eleanor Neale smiled broadly. "Told you," she said.

I turned. She stood behind me, clothes flung on like the rest of us, hair tousled and down to her shoulders, brown eyes wide and startled as they saw my face, registered the tears, which were already streaming down my cheeks.

"Holly! Oh, Holly!" I swept her into my arms, almost crushing her in my embrace. "I thought – thought -oh, dear Lord, I'm so glad you're safe!"

"Aidan -?" She could only squeeze out my name, because I was holding her so tightly. "What is it? Why were you so -?"

"Worried?" I cut in. "Because I thought it might be you!" I nodded over my shoulder to where everyone was gathered round the tarpaulin.

I saw then that she was crying too. "Oh, Aidan I'm so sorry. I should have waited, told you where I was going. I didn't think. The shouts woke me, and my first thought was to find out what had happened."

"It doesn't matter," I croaked. "Nothing matters except that you're here – and I'm just so relieved."

We stood together in a clinch. How good it felt to hold her close, to know that she was safe, to feel relief washing over me with all the power of a gigantic wave. Just the two of us alone, for Eleanor had moved diplomatically forward to stand on the edge of the crowd.

Voices rumbled in the background. "Too much drink, I dare say." PC Curtis spoke with genuine regret.

Irene Pake sounded cold and dispassionate. "Came in the pub late on. I'd banned him that afternoon, but back he came, bent on trouble. He started arguing the toss with Bet here and wouldn't leave when I told him. Snowy and some others threw him out."

"Bet and me saw him when we left," Snowy said. "He was drunk as a lord, sitting on one of these here benches, feeling sorry for himself." Other voices piped up, confirming that they'd seen him too.

"So, I'd guess he eventually got up and fell in the water once everybody had gone home," Curtis decided.

"Well, that's what must've happened, because after I'd locked up, I didn't hear a thing," Irene Pake put in. "Though I'll tell you what, Bob. He and that young Hambling had a right barney down here yesterday lunchtime. The boy threatened to kill him and nearly choked the life out of him on the spot."

"I wouldn't read too much into what Edward said, Irene," Snowy mumbled cautiously.

"He *said* it," Irene insisted. "Exactly that. And you heard him, Snowy. So did Bet and one or two others." There were several nods and grunts of assent.

Curtis sighed. "S'pose I'd better get along to the Manor and talk to him, then," he said resignedly. He raised his voice. "Right, Irene and Snowy, I'll have a word with you first. Back home, the rest of you. Nothing more to see."

The crowd began to disperse, the fishermen heading for their boats. An ambulance had arrived, and Curtis and the doctor went to speak to the crew.

Holly and I had turned in alarm on hearing Irene's words. They'd sounded like an accusation. "Poor Edward," Holly muttered. "Aidan, you don't believe he could have -?"

Eleanor re-joined us before we could speculate further. "Let's get back and make that tea," she said. "Nothing we can do for Mr Delverton now. He might not have been a nice man, but I wouldn't have wished that on anyone. God rest his soul."

We returned to Harbour Heights, Eleanor leading at pace, Holly and I wandering back hand in hand. The ladies had dressed and were waiting downstairs, eager for news, but were immediately chastened when they learned what had happened and to whom. They sat drinking their tea in a sombre, reflective mood.

We'd only been back half-an-hour when the phone rang in reception, jarring us out of our torpor. Eleanor went and answered it, returning to the lounge, where we were all sitting, with a grim smile.

"For you, Mr Verney," she said. "I wondered how long it'd take her."

I went and picked up the receiver, aware that Eleanor wasn't far away, making a show of straightening the tablecloths in the dining room.

"Hello? Mr Verney?" I was surprised by the caller's tone: gushing yet holding a plea. "This is Ruth Bayldon. I've got Curtis, the Paxham constable, with me, questioning my grandson about an incident which he claims took place yesterday. Apparently, yourself and Miss Tasker witnessed it. I'd be so obliged if the two of you could come to the Manor and speak on Edward's behalf...You will? That'd be so kind. I'll expect you shortly."

I returned to the lounge, Eleanor at my heels, and spoke to Holly. She agreed to come with me. We took our leave of the ladies, confident that Eleanor would apprise them of the situation.

*

PC Curtis's Panda was parked outside the front door of the Manor. As we walked up the drive, I sensed that we were being watched and, sure enough, the door swung open before I could knock. Ruth Bayldon had been looking out for us.

She thanked us for coming so promptly and stood back to admit us. She seemed less formidable than previously, appearing a little stooped, her manner anxious, as she led us through to the bleak drawing room, where she'd taken me to task the other evening. The circumstances were different now.

Bob Curtis was a big man but, standing uniformed in front of the empty fireplace, he looked huge and forbidding. Edward, in a dressing-gown over his pyjamas, sat on the sagging sofa facing him, listlessly examining the threadbare carpet beneath his feet.

"Ah, Mr Verney, Miss Tasker," Curtis welcomed us. "Mrs Bayldon asked that you should come here to back up Mr Hambling's version of events."

103

I expected an interruption from Ruth over Curtis's words, but she remained silent, taking up a position behind Edward and merely spearing the constable with a resentful glare. I imagined she'd already vented her anger in words.

Curtis, however, seemed oblivious to it, his attention centred on Holly and me. We hadn't been invited to sit and stood just inside the room, facing him.

"Now, I believe you were both present at the altercation outside the Lobster Pot yesterday lunchtime between Mr Hambling and the deceased? I've already interviewed Snowy Neale and Irene Pake, but I'd like you to tell me in your own words what the quarrel was about?"

"It's a conspiracy, that's what it is!" Ruth Bayldon broke in viciously. "They're all in it against him, spreading rumours and deliberately upsetting the boy to make him ill. How many more times do I have to tell you?"

Curtis held up a hand. "Please, Mrs Bayldon. I need to hear Mr Verney's and Miss Tasker's version of events. The others have simply told me what they *saw*. They've no axe to grind against Mr Hambling."

Ruth Bayldon folded her arms imperiously and glared back at him with contempt.

"So, Mr Verney?" Curtis resumed.

I exchanged a glance with Holly. "I think I can speak for us both?" She assented with a nod.

Edward looked up at me briefly and then away. He looked disconsolate, as if what I might be about to say would be of no help to him. I wasn't sure that he appreciated the seriousness of the situation.

"As I understand it," I said, "Mr Delverton was some sort of property developer, and he wanted to purchase a field which belongs to the Manor. Mrs Bayldon was totally against selling it, so Delverton tried to bully Edward into getting her to change her mind. He made an offer, which Edward rejected.

"Holly and I witnessed Delverton putting him under a lot of unfair pressure and, quite honestly, I felt he pushed him too far. It came to blows, and Snowy Neale and I had to restrain Edward. Edward threatened Delverton, but it was in the heat of the moment. I don't wish to speak ill of the dead, but Delverton seemed to have the knack of getting under anyone's skin, particularly if things didn't go his way. Irene Pake sent him packing, we helped to calm Edward down and, shortly afterwards, he went home. That was about it."

Curtis nodded. "And you confirm what he's just said, Miss Tasker?" he asked.

"That's exactly as I remember it, Mr Curtis," Holly replied.

Ruth Bayldon barged in, determined to have her say. "Yes, constable. Edward arrived back here yesterday afternoon, terribly upset. He told me he'd had words with Delverton, then went up to his room. I didn't see him again before dinner."

"Might he have gone out later?" Curtis suggested.

"I certainly didn't," Edward struck in peevishly.

Ruth was right behind him. "And I'd have heard if he had. I sleep lightly, when at all, and didn't in fact go to bed until after one p.m."

As Curtis was noting this down, it occurred to me that Ruth had said nothing about Delverton's visit to the Manor late the previous afternoon. I guessed I'd been the only person to have witnessed that.

"Doctor reckons time of death to have been either side of midnight," Curtis said.

"Then clearly my grandson could have had nothing to do with it," Ruth snapped. "You're wasting your time, constable."

Curtis let her comments go but looked far from convinced. "Irene Pake tells me Delverton tried to gain entry to the Lobster Pot just before closing," he went on. "Even though she'd banned him from there after the incident at lunchtime. He was rolling drunk, and she pitched him out on his ear. That was the last she saw of him, though when Snowy Neale and his lady friend left, they saw him sitting on one of the benches outside, looking sorry for himself. One or two who left about the same time have confirmed that."

"Then that was the last time anyone saw him alive," Ruth Bayldon declared impatiently. "Clearly, the wretched man was so drunk, that when he got up, he must have walked straight over the edge of the quay."

Curtis grunted unhappily, looked around and thanked us all, before taking his leave. Ruth Bayldon followed him to the door, and we heard her continuing to berate him, as he went out to his car.

Edward got to his feet and came towards us. "Thank you for backing me up," he said. "It was decent of you." He offered a hand, cold and damp, which I shook.

"I don't believe you could have killed him, anyway," I said. Edward had certainly been in a murderous rage only hours earlier, but I couldn't see him trailing after Delverton and waiting around the quay all evening, before pushing him into the water.

Holly leaned forward to hug him, as he turned towards her, but he simply offered a formal hand, which she took with a hint of coolness.

We heard PC Curtis drive away, and Ruth Bayldon returned to the room. She thanked us again, now reverting to her accustomed manner, and indicated for Edward to see us to the door. We said goodbye and left.

We'd served our purpose.

24

We returned to Harbour Heights, where Eleanor had prepared us a cooked breakfast. The ladies were just finishing theirs and were in deep discussion. They seemed lacklustre, and I wondered if the morning's events had knocked them out of their cosy stride.

With breakfast over, Holly returned to chambermaid duties, and later in the morning I called in at the Lobster Pot. The pub was sparsely populated, and the mood sombre. Clarence Darby, who never stayed long into the evening, had heard about the tragedy from Snowy that morning and condemned it as an unfortunate accident.

"The poor man must have had something weighing on his mind to have allowed himself to get as drunk as that."

"Ah, the landlord at the Boatman said he was in roistering form yesterday evening," Snowy said. "Not when he barged his way in here, though. He was determined to be obnoxious and upset Bet something rotten."

106

Irene Pake was polishing glasses behind the bar. "She's got no backbone, that one," she growled, throwing Snowy an unfavourable look. "Good job she's off today, otherwise she'd have all you daft men sympathising and fussing around her."

"I should say she's got a bit more spirit than you give her credit for," Snowy retorted. He buried his nose in his tankard, avoiding the savage glance Irene directed at him. "As for Delverton, I couldn't stand the bloke, and he brought it on himself. But I'm sorry it happened, all the same."

I stayed there for a sandwich and a shandy, but Snowy seemed a shadow of his usual jovial self, and Clarence quite subdued. However, neither of them felt that Edward Hambling could have been responsible for Delverton's death.

"Wouldn't have had it in him," was Irene's disparaging assessment. "Although I dare say that old cat of a grandma would. No, it was the drink that did for friend Delverton, particularly seeing the amount he put away."

My next call was to the police house, where I found PC Curtis sifting through witness statements. But he welcomed me in and poured us each a mug of tea, strong and stewed, from a large stainless steel tea pot.

"You here to add something to what you've already given me, Mr Verney?" he asked. "Seems pretty much cut and dried, if you ask me."

"Exactly what they're saying down at the Lobster Pot," I replied. "No, I'm just curious about Tony Delverton. He wasn't my idea of a property developer."

"Mine neither," Curtis grinned. "But he was the sort who'd wheel and deal his way through everything. I've been on the blower to his local nick in London, 'cause I was sure they'd be interested in him. He's got a bit of form, though nothing recent. He was a slippery customer, keeping an office in Walworth, which they were aware of. Not that he kept anything incriminating there. No, their opinion was, that he was careful; and they reckon he was pretty much on his uppers, snatching at any opportunity that came his way.

"Here's a strange thing, though. At one time, he was married to Valerie Kaye."

Curtis's tone was one of awe, as if I ought to know the name. "Sorry? Valerie who?"

"Ah, of course, you'd be too young to have heard of her. She was a singer, lad. Very big in London during the war years. Not quite up there with Vera Lynn, Gracie Fields and the like but, my, she could belt 'em out. *Happy Return* and *My Heart's Gone with my Soldier*. Got married and dropped out of sight. Though it beats me how a lovely lass like her could get took in so easy by a con artist like him.

"Young Edward Hambling's decent enough," Curtis went on. "Bit gullible, but Mrs Bayldon never let him mix with ordinary folk. Still, it's well known they're in need of money at the Manor, so you can imagine the lad in two minds over Delverton's line of patter." The constable chuckled caustically. "No flies on his grandma, though."

"So, Edward's off the hook?"

Curtis blew out his cheeks. "Nothing more to be said, after Mrs Bayldon vouched for him. The coroner's one of her bridge set, and you know how these toffs stick together. He'll be satisfied Delverton's death was an accident."

I was happy to learn that I shouldn't be needed to give evidence or a character reference at the impending inquest. I gave the constable my address and home telephone number, telling him I'd be away from Paxham for a few days. As I'd hoped, he accepted that without question.

It was mid-afternoon when I arrived back at Harbour Heights, sensing the gloomy atmosphere the moment I walked in. Eleanor and Holly were in the lounge, drinking tea and looking doleful.

Holly threw me a tired smile. "Don't look now, Miss Neale. But our last remaining guest has just returned."

"Last?" I frowned. "Have the ladies gone?"

"Left this lunchtime," Eleanor said. There was a third cup on the tray before her, and she poured me some tea. "I could tell they were fidgety when I gave them the news about Mr Delverton this morning. They sat there in a huddle over breakfast, went up to their room for a while and came down full of apologies. Apparently, one of 'em's got a cousin in Exeter, and they reckoned they couldn't put off seeing her any longer. So, they paid up, quick as you like, and toddled off."

"Couldn't get away fast enough if you ask me," Holly put in.

"Two deaths in a week," Eleanor sighed. "If this don't close us down, I don't know what will." She reached across and patted my hand. "At least you're still with us, dear."

"Ah."

They both looked up sharply, Holly appearing particularly taken aback.

"Not you as well, Mr Verney?" Eleanor groaned.

"I phoned home earlier." I'd come back that afternoon, having rehearsed the lie. "Mum's gone down with 'flu and Dad's on night shift, so someone needs to keep an eye on Grandad. Hopefully, I'll just be away a couple of nights."

"Then you're coming back?" I felt lifted by the note of expectation in Holly's voice. Eleanor looked away with a sly grin.

"Yes, I'll be back." I sensed my face reddening. "I've just checked with PC Curtis: he's sure I won't be needed at the inquest. Are you happy to keep the room on for me, Miss Neale? And is it okay to leave some of my stuff here?"

I was afraid that she was about to kiss me. "That's absolutely *fine,* Mr Verney. And, of course, there's no problem about the room. Well, not now, anyway. You're not going this afternoon?"

"I was planning to catch the nine-thirty in the morning."

She clapped her hands together almost gaily, leaving Holly looking bemused. "Then you'll have time for a decent breakfast, and tonight the three of us'll sit and have our meal together." She beamed at us both. "I'm sure Holly won't object to that."

It was Holly's turn to blush, and she stood up. "I'd better get on with the veg, then."

"And I'll get out from under your feet," I decided. I wanted some time alone, to put my thoughts in order.

The afternoon had turned cloudy, and a breeze had sprung up, but I found the walk invigorating. It was only as I was returning to the hotel that the name PC Curtis had mentioned popped into my mind.

Valerie Kaye.

Delverton had been married to Valerie Kaye. And the woman who'd visited him at the hotel, from whom he'd tried to borrow money: he'd called her Val and tried to pass her off as his sister.

The same woman?

I added her to my list. I was suddenly keen to track her down.

25

After breakfast the next morning, I pitched a few necessary items into my duffel bag and went down to reception to settle my bill to date. Eleanor had assured me there was no need, as I'd be coming back anyway, but I insisted, knowing that in the light of recent events this must be a thin time for her.

"Well, we shall miss you," Eleanor remarked. "It's been a help and a pleasure to have you around. Let's hope the sea air's done you some good."

It occurred to me then that I'd had so much on my mind, I'd given little thought to the matter of my illness.

As I was finishing off with Eleanor, Holly put her head round the kitchen door. "All right if I walk down to the station with Aidan, Miss Neale?" she asked.

I caught Eleanor's knowing grin before she could turn away. "Ah, I wondered if you might want to do that," she murmured, before giving Holly her permission in a louder voice.

We set off, walking a little way in silence, before Holly broke in tentatively. "You've not been well, have you? Nelly mentioned the other day that you've not long come out of hospital. Were you very ill?"

"It was cancer," I replied, amazed at how effortless it was to speak the word; and how casual, making it sound on a par with measles or tonsillitis.

"Oh, Aidan." Her hand snatched at my arm, bringing us to a halt. "I had no idea." She stared at me aghast, her eyes bright with pity.

"They caught it early," I went on, striving to reassure her. "And I'm feeling a whole lot better than a few weeks ago. The diagnosis is good." *No guarantees,* they'd said, because with cancer there never were. I didn't wish to worry her with that. "The sea air's helping." I smiled down at her. "Other things too."

She smiled back, linking her arm through mine. "I'm glad. And if you should want to talk, you know where to find me."

"Yes, yes. We need to talk." I guessed she'd read the urgency in my response, for I immediately felt her tense. We walked on in silence, and I feared she might have gone back into her shell.

But soon, she spoke again. "Aidan, you don't think that, after all, it might have been that Edward pushed Delverton off the quay?"

"No, Holly, I don't. Why do you ask?"

"He's so hung up, it's impossible to get through to him. He seems to feel everyone's against him."

"I can understand that." I was revisited by the images of the hospital ward, so drab and sanitised, of Diana coming to visit on that fateful day, so uptight that I'd known something was badly wrong. I'd been at a low ebb anyway. But her news had plunged me to such depths as I'd never known before. It had been sudden, final; world-shattering. I'd felt so weak and defeated; so isolated.

Holly seemed to sense my mood and tugged on my arm, bringing me back to the here and now. I was touched by her concern for me.

"You're on your way home," she said. "Where's that, exactly?"

"It's a small market town near Oxford, famous for blanket making. Nothing much ever happens."

"Which is probably why you're not going there now. Because you're not, are you? And your mum's not ill?"

I scrutinised her face closely. Despite her anxiety, she was smiling mysteriously, and I found myself looking at her in a new light. How had she reached that conclusion? Was I so easy to read, or was she more alert, more perceptive than I'd given her credit for?

"And there I was, thinking I'd been so clever," I grinned. "But you're right on both counts."

111

"So, where are you going?"

"London."

"Why?"

I had to confide some of what I suspected. In a way, I was glad to, because I felt deeply disturbed, sensing that I stood on the edge of a mystery. I was certain the answer didn't lie in Paxham, and that I had to go out and unearth it.

"You see, Holly, I'm sure that both Tony Delverton and Connie Instow fit into this somewhere."

She stared back incredulously.

"She recognised Delverton," I went on. "And he recognised her, even though he denied it when I asked him the other day."

"Do you think he might have killed her?" Her voice was a whisper.

"I don't know. But one thing I do know: the woman who had tea with him at the hotel the other day, the woman he told us was his sister – I believe she's actually his ex-wife."

"So, you're saying there's a connection between them all?"

"Possibly. And they're all from London. I wonder if the answer might lie there."

"London's a big place."

Connie Instow's words came back to me in a flash. I felt invigorated, took them as a sign, as I repeated them. "Yes, but it's a small world."

I asked Holly to keep my confidence, and she promised she would, looking at me with something akin to awe. I felt astonished by it; humbled too. I didn't feel there was anything remotely awesome about me: no job prospects, a big question mark over my life prospects, and otherwise ordinary in every way. But I was glad, too, felt I might somehow be teetering on the verge of happiness.

Apart from those shadows. Always, it seemed, those shadows...

We reached the station. I purchased my ticket, and she came with me on to the platform. I told her I was going to visit General Hambling first.

"Edward told me he's rather gaga," Holly said. "He finds it difficult making conversation. I don't know how much help the general will be."

"I'll give it a try, anyway. Once I've found the care home where he lives. It's on the outskirts of Eastbourne, isn't it?"

"I can help you there. I once saw a letter the warden had written to Edward. It's the Gresley Care Home in Seascape Road. Edward usually catches a bus from the station." Suddenly, she was anxious again. "Aidan? Do you think there's anything in that rumour – that Edward is really Georgie Kell? The whole village seems to be talking about it, and that'll upset Edward even more."

"For Edward's sake, I hope that it's just a malicious rumour."

The train bustled in, squealing to a halt.

"Aidan – take care."

Her grip on my arm tightened, and she looked up, her eyes wide and pleading. There was something forlorn and vulnerable about her. She seemed to want to ask me something yet was preventing herself from doing so. And the question could only come from her.

There was a moment's hesitation, before she flung herself into my arms and I held her close again, feeling myself fired by that contact, by her dependence on me. I wondered, if, somehow, that was what I'd become: her lifeline. It was a peculiar thought; but I couldn't shake it away.

We kissed, and a procession of memories slalomed across my mind. Diana, the last girl I'd kissed like this; Diana, who'd abandoned me, who'd walked away. *"I'm sorry, Aidan, but, you see, I – I've met someone else…"* And leaving me in tears, in utter, abject misery in my hospital bed.

How I wanted this, now, with Holly, to be my redemption. If only it could be! If only those mysterious shadows weren't there, skulking along the way ahead, waiting to ambush and engulf us in their darkness.

We drew apart reluctantly, as the guard's whistle sounded. I scrambled on to the train, wound down the window. We clasped hands, but the jolting of the train tore them apart. She blew me kisses, waved, and I leaned out of the window, waving back, until the train rounded the bend, and she was lost to sight.

I found a compartment and sat down in a daze. Swathes of countryside wafted past, towns, villages, fields and farms. I noticed none of these, for my thoughts were all for her. I felt fortified by her, as if I could at last stow away ever hurtful memory of that ghastly preceding year. But I knew I could only do so for a while; and I wanted to live in and savour those last sweet moments for as long as possible.

I tried to focus on the task ahead. I'd go to Eastbourne first, hoping to get some answers from General Hambling. I'd been prepared to trawl around every care home in the town, but Holly had bailed me out: the Gresley Care Home in Seascape Road. And then I sat for a while and prayed to a God, who, from my childhood, I'd believed was there and would understand; that all could and would be well.

I sat up with a start, as Connie's image came to mind: Connie, barely conscious, breathing those final words.

Of course. The word she'd uttered hadn't been 'Lessley'.

It had been *'Gresley.'*

26

Gresley Care Home was situated outside Eastbourne with views of the busy Channel before it, the sprawl of the town in one direction and the coastline leading along to Beachy Head in the other. It was an imposing Victorian mansion, with single-storey extensions to the side and rear, its prim, white façade in contrast to the front garden enlivened by rudbeckia, chrysanthemum and dahlia, a wide expanse of well-tended lawn spilling down to the sea, criss-crossed by paths which wove in and out of little clusters of trees and bushes.

It was late afternoon when I arrived. The receptionist looked doubtful when I asked to see General Hambling. She rang a bell on the desk, and, within a few seconds, a plain but kindly-looking woman emerged from an office along the corridor and came towards me. She introduced herself as Mary Lockhart, the warden.

I told her that I'd been on holiday in Paxham and had got to know Edward, the general's grandson. He was preparing for a recital and, knowing I'd been heading this way, had asked if I'd mind looking in on the general and phoning to let him know how he was.

Mary Lockhart frowned. "General Hambling's very frail and tends to get easily upset. Edward was down here only the other day, but I can understand that he's concerned about his grandfather. I don't think a few minutes will do any harm, but please, try to keep it brief. I'll go along and fetch him. What name shall I say?"

"Aidan Verney. But he won't know me."

"Right. Let me show you to the lounge, and I'll bring General Hambling along there."

Somehow, I'd convinced the warden that my reason for calling was genuine. But I felt uncomfortable with the deception, because it went against my better judgement. Mary Lockhart took me a little way along the corridor to where it opened out into a large area dotted with armchairs and coffee tables. A few residents sat there, gazing out through the patio window over the rear garden to the sea.

"General Hambling's *so* proud of his grandson," she said. "He nearly lost him in the early days. He's the only relative the general has left, and he looks so contented when Edward gives a little piano recital to the residents. Such a talented young man."

I took a seat, while she hurried off to find the general. Several minutes elapsed before she reappeared, pushing him along in a wheelchair. I promptly stood to greet him and was disturbed by what I saw, for before me sat a near-skeletal version of the man whose photograph I'd seen at the Manor a few nights previously. He wore a dark blazer with a double row of medals: they seemed to drag him down further in his chair.

It was a sunny day, and sunlight shone directly in the general's face as Mary Lockhart brought him in. The old man was unable to distinguish my features and suddenly howled in anguish.

"That jacket! It's him – back again! How *dare* you let him in here! Send him away! I refuse to speak to him!"

The residents present looked on in alarm. But their shock was nothing to that of mine and Mary Lockhart's.

She quickly took control, suggesting that I moved round a little to enable the general to see that I was a complete stranger.

"Look, General Hambling, Mr Verney's a much younger man. The other one won't come back. We know not to let him in. Mr Verney's a friend of your grandson,

115

Edward, who's asked him to look in on you, because he's not able to come himself at present."

She explained all this in a gentle tone, as if trying to reason with a child and, as the old man obtained an unhampered look at me, he calmed down. I took an uncertain step forward, hand extended, uncomfortably aware of Mary Lockhart studying me closely.

"Good afternoon, General Hambling. My name's Aidan Verney. How do you do?"

The general grunted and offered a limp hand, which I shook with great care. "How is Edward?" His voice was like a snarl, giving me a glimpse of yellow, decaying teeth.

"He's well." The old man lifted a tetchy hand to his ear, and I raised my voice. "He couldn't come himself. He's preparing for a recital."

"Huh, thought that was last week," the general barked. "So it was, confound it!"

"Er, this is another one." I could sense Mary Lockhart's probing gaze on my hot face, but I ploughed on. "General Hambling, I realise that a lot of the time you were away on military service, but you've known Edward since he was a baby, haven't you?"

I feared I'd formed the question clumsily but was pleasantly surprised when the old man's face seemed to clear. He was probably smiling, but it appeared more like a grimace. I guessed he'd been a hard man, a stranger to humour. The warden had mentioned the general's pride, and I felt I was witnessing it now. Before me was the result of his pride: a near-helpless wreck, languishing in a care home, all past glories fled.

"He was born soon after the death of my son," he chanted. "A true hero, who died a soldier's death."

"I've been told he greatly resembles his father?"

I'd been told nothing of the sort. I was fishing for a reaction, and Hambling's misty gaze seemed far away, peering down into the well of memory.

"There are certain features, naturally. After the boy's mother died, Bayldon packed him off to a decent school, with my blessing. I was away in Korea, only saw the boy once in a while. He'll never be a soldier, but a talented pianist, for sure. Mark my words, he'll be great one day."

116

"Did you see much of him before he went away to school?"

"See him? Confound it, of course I didn't see him! I was a soldier, man, serving King and country. Left the Bayldons to bring up the boy. Couldn't have him tagging along after me." He paused, and in that brief silence seemed to sink deeper in the wheelchair, weighed down by his medals and memories.

"I kept in touch, of course," he went on. "The Hambling line must continue. The Bayldons were as committed to that as I was. To think how we almost lost that boy..." He looked confused, staring past me as if I wasn't in the room. "I don't know how I'd have borne that loss. Not so soon after my son's death. We are a proud family, and the line must go on. It *must. I demand it...*"

He choked on a loud sob, began coughing, a hollow, racking noise. He flapped a dismissive hand at me, the room and everyone in it.

Mary Lockhart turned the chair round. "I'll take him back," she whispered. "You'll get nothing more from him."

I nodded ruefully. "I'd be grateful if you and I could have a word, though?"

"Oh, yes." Again, the probing gaze. "Yes, I think we should. Wait here, while I settle him."

I watched with pity, as General Hambling was wheeled away. An old man, who clung to the last vestige of his pride; but tormented, frail and broken inside.

It was close on twenty minutes later, when Mary Lockhart reappeared, bearing a tea tray, which she set down on the table between us. She pulled up a chair and poured tea in a brisk, purposeful manner.

Her smile, as she handed me a cup, convinced me that she'd seen through my feeble ruse. She might, justifiably, have been angry. But, fortunately for me, she was the epitome of calm.

"Edward Hambling didn't send you, did he?" she said discreetly.

"No, he didn't," I replied readily. "But I assure you that I know him and have been staying in Paxham."

She held up a hand. "Oh, I'm sure that's the case. And although I don't understand your reason for coming here, I'm sure it's nothing sinister. But you asked a

117

particular question which puzzled me. Of course, General Hambling's known Edward all his life. Why wouldn't he?"

I was hopeless at deception: something which had always gone against the grain with me. And there was no point in trying to fence with Mary Lockhart.

I explained that I'd been on holiday in Paxham, and that Miss Neale, proprietress of Harbour Heights Hotel, could vouch for me. I'd become friendly with Edward (although as I said it, I realised I was stretching a point) and, even though I couldn't go into details, rumours were going around the village about the validity of Edward's inheritance.

Mary Lockhart looked scandalised. "Oh, how awful! I can understand that Edward must be extremely upset."

"The rumours are really getting to him," I said. "I came here to see General Hambling in the hope that he might know something which would utterly overturn them."

She shook her head sadly. "You can see the state he's in. He's confused and not in a good way. He'd be of no help to you. Besides, I'm not sure he'll be around much longer. It was only yesterday that we had to call in the doctor again. He said to prepare ourselves for the worst. In the past few weeks, the general's become increasingly agitated, hard to settle and persistently refusing to take his medication."

"He was certainly confused when he saw me," I recalled. "He said something about a man who came here?"

"Oh, the general surpassed himself that day, and he's been going steadily downhill since. Of course, with the sun in his eyes, he couldn't see your face."

"He only saw my denim jacket." A recollection flashed across my mind. Denim jackets were common enough, but I remembered another man whom I'd seen wearing one recently. "I don't suppose you can describe the man who came here and upset him so badly?" I asked tensely.

"Oh, I shan't forget him in a hurry. It must have been about three weeks ago." As soon as she launched into a description, I knew I was on the right track.

Because the man she described was Tony Delverton.

27

"I might have known there was going to be trouble," Mary Lockhart went on, "when the bell rang at reception, and I came out to find him standing there, asking to see General Hambling. I hesitated before replying. The general isn't good with visitors, and this made two in quick succession. His grandson's the only one he'll tolerate.

"I didn't take to the man from the moment I saw him. He'd been flirting with my receptionist and straightened up when he saw me approaching. I put him at around fifty, but with his bronzed face, denim jacket and garish shirt, he was trying to pass himself off as younger. I asked what his business was with the general. I doubted that he was a relative and was afraid he might have turned up with a view to trying to sell the poor man something. He said his name was Tony Dalton.

"He'd greeted me with a big smile and firm handshake, but then his expression became serious. Could we have a private word, he asked? It was a very delicate matter.

"I brought him through to the lounge. There were a few residents sprinkled around, but no-one within earshot. I wanted to leave him in no doubt that, if he wasn't above board, he'd have to get past me first.

""I'm here on a mission of mercy, Mrs Lockhart," he said, once we were seated. "I've come on behalf of a relative of General Hambling, who's fallen on hard times."

""Surely, you can't mean Edward?" I was shocked, Mr Verney. The young man had only been here the previous week. He'd played some pieces for his grandfather and a few other residents. It was good to see the general listening contentedly – made a change to him flying off into one of his rages.

"Mr Dalton shrugged. "I wouldn't know anything about an Edward," he said. "You see, I'm not acquainted with the general or any of his family. But, well, my sister happens to be his son's widow."

""But I understood that she was dead?" I exclaimed. "She was Edward's mother, and I forget her name. She'd been widowed in the War and died in a ferry accident not long afterwards."

"His face broke into a smile, as he shook his head. "Ah, I can see why you're puzzled. No, there was another son, who also died in the War: my sister's husband. They weren't wed for long. And my sister, bless her, never remarried, always dedicated to honouring her husband's memory. It's just that she's been ill for some time." He paused and ran a hand over his face: he appeared quite distraught. "I just wish she'd told me earlier. I've been working in South Africa – a mining engineer – and I've only just got back. She's on her uppers and in need of expensive treatment. Way beyond my means, I'm afraid. I've a young family to support and, well, we talked, and I agreed to come and ask General Hambling if he might be able to help her out a little..."

"I can tell you, Mr Verney, I felt torn. The man seemed sincere enough, but I couldn't say I altogether trusted him. Yet I didn't feel I could turn him away.

"I told him the general was very tired. He'd already had one visitor that morning, and it hadn't turned out well. I said I'd let Mr Dalton have a few minutes with him, but I insisted on being on hand and would curtail the interview, if necessary. With General Hambling's delicate state of health, I wasn't willing to take any chances.

"Dalton's mouth tightened, and I noticed that the expression in his eyes was hard. I wondered if he'd thought I'd be a soft touch. But his face quickly cleared, as he realised this was the only opportunity he'd get. He thanked me and said a few minutes would be all he'd need. The smile was back – on his face, at least.

"I went and fetched General Hambling. Dalton leapt up as we approached, wearing an ingratiating smile. I crouched down beside the general and introduced his visitor. "He realises it's nearly your lunchtime, so he won't keep you long." If there's one thing General Hambling hates, it's a break in his routine, and we've been taken to task for that more than once, since he's been here.

"I directed a warning glance at Dalton, but I don't think it registered with him, because his whole attention was for the general. He offered a hand and looked put out when it was ignored. I already had the uncomfortable feeling that this wouldn't go well.

"Mr Dalton patiently explained the reason for his visit, repeating everything he'd told me. The general appeared unmoved, not bothering to make eye contact. Then Dalton said something along the lines of 'she's your son Freddie's widow,' that it was a matter of life and death, and he'd be more than happy to take a cheque on her behalf, even if it was just for a few hundred pounds...

"I'd been standing to the side and by then wishing I'd turned the man away. I still thought the case was genuine, but he was sounding increasingly desperate, and his words had, for me, something of a hollow ring.

"So far, General Hambling had said nothing and hadn't even indicated that he'd been listening, but suddenly his breath started coming in ragged gasps. Then his hands and arms began to quiver, and his torso to shake. I realised with horror that he was struggling to escape from his wheelchair. I tried to calm him, but he paid me no attention.

""GET OUT!" he bawled, and Dalton leapt in alarm. "Blast you, get out NOW!" He tried to stand, only succeeding in slithering further down in his seat, his feet pounding the floor and a shuddering finger aimed at the door, dismissing his visitor. He yelled at the top of his voice that 'that man' had been no son of his. He refused to call him by his name. He'd married some chorus girl to spite his father, and the general had disowned him. He wouldn't listen to another word. My goodness, did he rant and rave! His language was foul.

"Dalton tried to protest but only managed to plunge him into a greater rage. A nurse and my receptionist hurried across and tried their best to calm him. I told them to take him back to his room, took Mr Dalton by the arm and led him away.

"I explained to him that he had to leave and not return. General Hambling was a sick man, and I couldn't allow him to be upset any further.

"I found myself pitying Dalton, for, whatever he'd been expecting, he hadn't bargained for this. He looked ill, allowing me to escort him to the door and bid him good day. I watched him slope away. He looked utterly defeated. Fortunately, he's never returned, which is just as well. It's given us the chance to settle the general back into his accustomed routine."

*

I'd listened, fascinated by the warden's narrative, and picked up something she'd mentioned in passing.

"Mrs Lockhart," I said, as, having drawn to a close, she poured us each some more tea, "you mentioned that General Hambling had already received one visitor that morning?"

"Yes. The lady. I'm wondering if Mr Dalton might have fared better if she hadn't called. Because her visit started everything off."

"What was she like?"

"Elderly, well-spoken, tidily dressed in a dark suit. She seemed a genuine sort of person. She did give her name, but it's escaped me for the moment."

"It wasn't Mrs Bayldon, Edward's grandmother?"

Mary Lockhart looked amused. "Oh, heavens, no. She only came down once, and the general took against her: far too gushing. I think he left her in no doubt that he didn't want her here again."

I could see his point; and was now fairly sure who the first visitor had been. "Might this lady by any chance have passed Mr Dalton on her way out?" I asked.

"Almost certainly. He arrived within minutes of her leaving. And I'm sure she didn't drive here. She'd probably have waited out on the pavement for a bus."

"Was her name Instow?"

Mary Lockhart clapped her hands. "That's it! Why, do you know her?"

There was that image of Connie Instow that I guessed I'd always retain: her head bowed in prayer in the little harbour chapel. A woman of faith, of compassion, who'd rejoiced in her gift of life and who'd died an untimely death...

"Yes. We stayed at the same hotel in Paxham. But I'm puzzled as to why she came here?"

"Well, she didn't go into detail. She said she was calling on behalf of one of the general's relatives and promised she'd only keep him a short while."

"How did she fare?"

"Badly. I overheard her saying something along the lines of him – presumably the relative – being very ill, and that he begged General Hambling's forgiveness. I wasn't present for the whole conversation, but I never heard her raise the question of money.

"Yet the general swore at her, and she recoiled in shock. He yelled that he refused to trade another word with her and then barked at the nurse to take him back to his room. I hurried over then. The lady was pleading with him, something about his 'own flesh and blood'. And she begged the general to try in his heart to forgive him.

"He paid no heed. She watched him go, thanked me, then turned and left. She looked very downcast."

"Then both she and Dalton were on the same mission," I said. "They were both talking about Freddie, the son the general had disowned?"

"They must have been," Mary Lockhart replied. "For a different purpose, perhaps, but they got the same reaction."

I thanked her for bearing with me. She replied that she hoped what I'd learned might be of some help to Edward. I hoped the same, but right at that moment didn't see how it could, and I left there with much on my mind.

Connie Instow and Tony Delverton had almost certainly recognised one another from their visit to Gresley Care Home.

I recalled the words Connie had murmured on the first occasion she'd encountered them at Harbour Heights. *"Surely – not the two of them?"*

If Delverton had been one, who might be the other?

28

I put up for the night in a cheap and cheerful B & B near the sea front, reached London mid-morning and made my way across the city to the address in Walworth printed on Tony Delverton's business card.

As I'd expected, it was hardly the nerve centre for business in the capital, a grimy, glass-fronted building of six floors. My footsteps echoed in the empty foyer, and a tired-looking sign announced that there were offices to let. I suspected there could be quite a few.

I ground up in the lift to the fifth floor to find myself in a narrow corridor with Sunstream Holidays on one side and Frenzo Games Inc on the other. The first door bore a hastily scrawled note which read 'Gone Away' and the second a dog-eared square of card with the message 'Out to Lunch. Back Soon' printed on it.

Delverton Enterprises occupied a small office at the end of the corridor, and I paused outside the door. I'd been curious to see the sort of environment in which Delverton had worked and having done so, wasn't surprised. But I also wanted to find any paperwork relating to Edward Hambling. Since the proposed deal was now redundant, I intended to take it back to Paxham and hand it over to Edward.

I'd also come there on the off chance, albeit a slim one, that Delverton might have employed a secretary, and that she might have been present, tidying up loose ends. I guessed it had been a fanciful notion: Delverton had had all the appearances of being a lone operator.

The door to the office stood partly open, and I stepped inside. Before me stood a desk, two office chairs and a battered dark green metal filing cabinet.

Suddenly, I heard a noise behind me, the faintest rustle of clothing. Anticipating a blow, I blundered forward to collide with the cabinet, caught my foot on its corner and went sprawling. By then, the figure had squeezed through the doorway and was scurrying off down the corridor, bequeathing a heady waft of perfume in its wake.

Scrambling to my feet, I set off in pursuit. At the end of the corridor, the lift stood empty. Turning the corner, I saw a fire exit, its swing door batting backwards and forwards on hinges which pined for oil. I peered down into the stairwell and glimpsed a dark-haired woman in a white mackintosh moving at speed some two or three floors down. I started to follow but quickly gave up. She'd be out on the street with several directions to choose from and should have no trouble shaking me off. However, Delverton's floor was now deserted, and I could take a good look around the office.

I went back there. The filing cabinet was practically empty, and paperwork was strewn across the desk. I noticed that the drawers were pulled out and went round the desk to examine them. Someone, I presumed it had been the woman, had tipped the whole office contents on to the desk. She must have been looking for something specific. I spent a few minutes sifting through papers but found nothing of interest. They consisted of bills and advertising junk, and I suspected that the cautious Delverton had kept anything that mattered in some other place, particularly if it pushed at the boundaries of legality.

As I emerged into the corridor, a chubby man in a loud blue suit was unlocking the door of the Frenzo Games office. He looked up as I approached.

"Not looking for Delverton, are you?" he inquired. "'Cause if so, he's -"

"Thanks," I interrupted. "I know." I might have added a lot more but didn't.

The man's face collapsed in a lop-sided grin. "Yeah, poor old boy. Local beat copper told me yes'day. Our Tone might have been a bit dodgy, but we had some laughs." He nodded towards the office I'd just vacated. "Owed you money, I expect? One or two have called in already. Won't find much there."

"I called in case he had a secretary."

Frenzo's laugh was deep and rumbling. "Would've kept the poor mare on her toes if he had. Nah, just Tone was all there was. Spent most of his time ducking and weaving, one step ahead of the law."

"You don't happen to know if he had another office?"

"So, he *did* owe you money?"

I shrugged. "Not a lot. But I thought if there might just be a chance -?"

There was a deal of cynicism in the lop-sided grin. "News to me if he had, although, in any case, he wouldn't have let on. Tell you what, chum. Anyone's likely to know, it'll be mine host and his missus at the Nine Bells. Down the end of the road and turn left. Can't miss it. Tone spent more time there than in his office. Reckoned he might strike it lucky with some barmaid. Always boasting he had a way with women. Well, that was how *he* told it."

I thanked Frenzo and left the building. I took the stairs, pondering on the woman who'd fled down them some twenty minutes before. A creditor, perhaps? Whatever she'd been looking for, I didn't think she could have found it.

The long bar of the Nine Bells was stocked with several varieties of every drink imaginable and a wide range of beers on tap. Posters of classic films of the 1940s and 50s enlivened the walls, the carpet a blaring orange and the seats brown vinyl.

Business was slack after lunch, and the licensees were happy to chat with me over my pie and shandy. He was large, bald and fiftyish, his stomach bulging dramatically beneath a riotous Hawaiian shirt, and she a diminutive bottle blonde with high hair and an array of glittering bangles and rings, which seemed to catch fire beneath the bar's fluorescent lighting.

They nodded ruefully when I asked if they knew Tony Delverton.

"Ah, we'll miss him. Profits'll be way down. In here a lot, weren't he, doll?"

She chuckled throatily and patted her skyscraper hair. "Oh, you bet. Weren't just the beer he was interested in."

125

The landlord arched his capacious eyebrows. "He was a lady's man right enough, with a smooth line of patter. Not that Olive here got taken in. Is it true what the Old Bill say? That he drowned somewhere in Devon?"

"A little place called Paxham," I replied. "Just along the coast from Leesbourne. He was staying in the same hotel as me. Apparently, one night he had a skinful and toppled off the quay."

The landlord laughed, and his wife indignantly slapped his arm. "Well," he protested, "it's the way he'd have wanted to go. Blimey, he lived life on the run, did Tony. He was into this and that. A likeable enough bloke, 'specially when he'd had a few. But you wouldn't trust him as far as you could throw him."

There seemed to be no flies on them, and I decided to probe a bit further, in the hope of finding out if Delverton had had an associate.

"You're right about his schemes," I said. "There's a young chap in Paxham, whose grandad's in a nursing home on the coast – a retired general, on his last legs and very rich. Delverton latched on to that and called in on the old chap a few weeks back, trying to tap him for some money. He claimed it was for his sister, who'd been married to one of the general's late sons."

The landlord was already shaking his head. "No relation of Tony would ever have been married to a general's son," he scoffed. "As for a sister, blowed if I ever heard him mention one. Did you, doll?"

"He never had no sister," she confirmed scornfully. "Always best to take anything he said with a generous pinch of salt. He opened up one night in here, when he'd had too many. Blimey, he was feeling sorry for himself. Told me he'd been brought up by Barnardo's, 'cause his mother had abandoned him at birth."

"Did he by any chance ever mention anyone named Val?"

"Yeah, he did, and not all that long ago. He said he was off down south, and if this Val came looking for him, to tell her he'd gone away on holiday."

"He owed her money," the landlord put in gravely. "Remember her, doll? Tidy-looking woman. I reckon it was about two weeks back. She looked real worried. He'd let slip some mention of this Paxham place, so I told her to try there."

"Trust you to fall for a pretty face," Olive scolded him.

"Well, she seemed a decent sort," he protested. "Felt I'd seen her somewhere before, but can't think where. Anyway, too decent to be taken for a mug by the likes of him. I hope she found him."

She had. I asked, and he obliged with a description of the woman who'd called on Delverton at Harbour Heights.

"Do you know of anyone else he was particularly friendly with?" I added.

They both laughed. "Practically every barmaid who ever worked here," he replied. "And that's just the Nine Bells. Ours wasn't the only place where he did his drinking, and he did plenty of that."

"There was one young girl he couldn't leave alone," Olive put in darkly. "Pretty little thing, and she wasn't keen on his crude advances. Friend of somebody he knew, as if that gave him the right to make such a nuisance of himself." Her husband looked blank, and she gave him a sharp dig in the ribs. "You *know*. The little blonde with the legs. The one you could never take your eyes off. Oh, what was her name, now? Molly? No – Holly. That was it. *Holly.*"

29

My head rang with the words uttered by Tony Delverton, as he'd sat at the bar in the Harbour Heights lounge, chatting up an unresponsive Holly. *"I looked at her and reckoned she'd pull a good pint..."*

The two licensees and the garish surrounds of the Nine Bells reduced to a blur, and their concerned voices echoed in my brain.

"Here, you all right, mate?"

"Get him a brandy quick, love. He's been took bad, gone all pale. Come on, dearie, come and sit down. Here, give us a hand..."

I was led, blundering, away from the bar and lowered on to one of the vinyl benches, glad of its support. I shook my head, trying to clear it, felt more focused after the first nips of brandy had kicked in.

Olive and her husband stood over me, their honest faces full of anxiety.

"I'm sorry about this," I apologised, babbling a little. "I'm just getting over an illness and guess I've been rushing around too much this morning. I'll be okay in a minute. *But I wondered if I would.*

The landlord went back to the bar to serve a customer, while Olive sat down beside me.

"Feel a bit better now, dearie?" she cooed.

"Yes, thanks. Just been overdoing things a little."

"It was the mention of the girl, wasn't it?" She was studying my face intently. "The girl who used to work here – Holly?"

I nodded limply. "I suppose it was. I – I know her, you see."

"Bit sweet on her too, I should reckon?" Olive smiled, displaying several gold fillings. "Got a nose for these things, y'know. But don't you go fretting. She was here less than six months. Think she'd been down on her luck a bit, but then a friend of hers had heard we needed a barmaid and sent her along. Our Tony used to badger her – oh, he was a terror if there was a pretty face involved. Anyway, one day somebody she knew phoned her up with another job offer, and she couldn't get away from here quick enough."

I thanked Olive for telling me all she had. She'd helped me over the initial shock, but the problem remained. I told her I ought to be moving on. I tried to pay for the brandy, but they wouldn't hear of it, wishing me the best of luck and inviting me to call back in, next time I was down their way.

The light breeze outside revived me further, but my mind was still reeling. I recalled Holly in my arms the previous morning at Paxham station, the way I'd felt, the sheer exhilaration. And the way I felt now: gutted, betrayed, Diana all over again.

If only Holly had told me she'd known Delverton. If only she could have trusted me, understood that I would never condemn her...

Always, that shadow, that foreboding of a darkness looming. Were there more secrets? Did Holly know Val as well? Had they and Delverton been in this together? I had to ask her, had to set my frantic mind at rest. But I felt loath to return to Paxham, knew I wasn't strong enough to face her yet. Before I could, there were things I had to do in London.

The afternoon was getting on by the time I found the address, a red-brick Victorian tenement, not far off Tower Bridge Road. I traipsed wearily up to the second floor but was heartened by the welcome lavished upon me by Billy Instow.

"Aidan, my *dear* boy! This is unexpected, but, by jingo, it's so good to see you! Come in, come in!"

He practically yanked me across the threshold and thrust me into an armchair. The apartment was dowdy but clean, the furniture elderly, although pride of place belonged to a large radiogram in walnut casing, and the piles of LPs and 78s stacked around and beneath it.

Billy bustled through to the little galley kitchen and brewed some tea, chattering away all the while.

"My, but they gave Con a good send-off down at Barber Street chapel. The little place was packed to the rafters, and the minister didn't half speak well of her. I was proud, I tell you, mighty proud."

He tried not to let me see that he had to wipe away a tear and attempted to cover his sorrow by stepping up the conversation, asking how things were with me, and" – here, he positively twinkled – "with that little girl at the hotel?"

I tried to put on a brave face, hoping my new-found anxiety wouldn't show. But Billy was no fool, and I was forced on to the defensive, hiding behind my slow ascent from illness and its consequent fatigue. Holly and I got on well, but I didn't want to rush into things.

Billy didn't press the issue. He was dressed in red blazer, white flannels and two-tone shoes, making me suspect that the inevitable straw boater was near to hand. His hair was slicked back with brilliantine and his moustache neatly trimmed. He was going out and urged me to accompany him.

"You look like you need cheering up, young man. So, come along with me, and we'll round off the evening with a fish-and-chip supper."

He explained that he was performing his regular slot at the Forever Companions Club a few streets away. The members were in their fifties and beyond, the songs from the thirties and forties, the beer and wine flowed, and a good dance and singalong were to be had by all.

In my gloom, I couldn't have felt less like going along to this or any other kind of entertainment. A polite disclaimer was on my lips, but Billy had welcomed me so generously and seemed – amazingly – enlivened by my presence.

So, I agreed, and he beamed, offering to put me up for the night. "The bed in the spare room's aired. Dear Con was forever nudging me to make sure I kept the place shipshape, and I've promised never to let her down anymore."

I thanked him, quietly relieved not to have to search around for a B & B that evening. I'd decided to stay away another night, because I still felt unable to face Paxham.

As I'd made my way across London that morning, I'd been dazzled by the sheer press of people and hectic pace of life; by the drooping moustaches, straggling hair, tunics, kaftans, maxi- and mini-skirts, beads and chains, the music blasting out of the many boutiques. The talk was of the recent Isle of Wight Festival and the headline acts of Hendrix, The Who and The Doors. I recalled the buzz which the Hyde Park Festival of the previous year had stirred up, even in my quiet hometown.

It was a new, perhaps exciting, certainly dizzying culture. But I remembered my grandad holding forth in a resonant voice, as he quoted an Old Testament passage, which proclaimed that there was nothing new under the sun.

This sprang into my mind, as Billy and I entered the function room of a large hotel near the waterfront, the territory of the Forever Companions Club, its walls lined with framed posters of artistes, bands and films from the war years, all celebrating a past culture. Many parallels could be drawn between the old and the new. Trends changed, disappeared only to return; but life moved relentlessly on.

On our arrival, a florid-faced man in a check suit and bowler hat was thumping out music hall songs on a grand piano on a small stage at the far end of the room. The audience, both men and women, ranging from middle-aged to elderly, were having a high time singing along with the pianist. Clothes were smart but garish: striped blazers, straw boaters, evening dresses and paste jewellery, the air fogged with smoke, tables creaking with tankards of beer, bottles of wine and imitation champagne, the atmosphere pulsating with nostalgia and merriment.

Billy seemed to know everyone, greeted with shouts and handshakes at every table we passed. A smiling waitress in a WAAF uniform took our orders for drinks, and Billy grinned at my surprise when he asked for nothing stronger than mineral water.

He waggled his fingers. "On in twenty minutes, lad," he said. "Need a clear head and steady hands." He winked mischievously. "I'll make up for it later, don't you worry."

The florid-faced man gave way to a trio of matrons, who serenaded the audience with what I was told were several Andrews Sisters numbers. Towards the end of their spot, Billy nudged me and announced that he'd better get backstage. I wished him luck but didn't think he'd need it, for he was entirely in his element.

A dapper little MC, in a white tuxedo which sported a red carnation, bustled on, as the curtain swished shut on the matrons, to announce with a flourish, "The man with the magic fingers, Mr Piano himself, ladies and gentlemen, I give you your own Mr – Billy – Instow!"

The curtains parted, and there sat Billy, the long-anticipated straw boater on his head, face split in a huge grin, as he launched into a medley of songs from World War 2. He was a lively and talented performer, who had the place jumping just a couple of numbers into his act. People were soon on their feet, clapping, dancing and chorusing along. Even I was able to forget my troubles for a while and be swept along on the tide of gaiety and goodwill.

After multiple bows, waves and two encores, the curtains closed on Billy, and an expectant hush descended on the room. In front of the stage, a quartet of musicians slipped into their seats and began tuning up. Once they were set, the MC reappeared.

"Ladies and gentlemen, none of our wonderful artistes will object if I call this the highlight of our evening. A beacon of light, which helped us through those dark days of war, a singer to be mentioned in the same breath as Vera Lynn and Gracie Fields. Ladies and gentlemen, I give you the lovely and unforgettable Miss – Valerie – Kaye!"

Thunderous applause followed the parting of the curtains, and a woman walked with practised sway to centre stage. She wore a glittering silver dress, jet-black hair sweeping down over her shoulders. Her face was masked with scarlet lipstick, rouge and eye shadow. But, even so, as I sat bolt upright in my seat and stared, I had no difficulty identifying the woman who'd called in on Tony Delverton at Harbour Heights and, I was sure, who'd fled from Delverton's office that very morning.

30

Valerie Kaye had worked her way through several numbers before Billy got back to me. He'd been joshing at the bar with a few cronies and now came swinging jauntily back, beer bottle in hand.

He nodded towards the stage. "The South London Lark," he sighed. "She's never lost it in my opinion. Any of it." Then he looked at me. "Blimey, boy. What's wrong? You seen a ghost or something?"

"I can't easily explain," I replied. "Billy, do you know Valerie Kaye?"

"*Know* her?" Billy was taken aback. "I've known her for years. Just wish I knew her better. A lovely lass, and always was."

"Can you ask her to join us once she's finished her act? Say a friend of yours wants to meet her?"

Billy hesitated, eyeing me curiously. "Obviously you've got your reasons, Aidan. I'll go along and nab her the minute she comes off stage."

Valerie Kaye finished to rapturous applause, and within a few minutes Billy was leading her over, having fetched her a glass of wine from the bar. People were still applauding and congratulating her as, looking bemused, she followed Billy on a tortuous course between the tables.

Billy pulled out a chair, which she took with a nervous smile.

"This is unusual. I didn't think anyone from the post-war generation would've heard of me." Then she saw me and immediately clamped a hand to her mouth. "Oh!"

I was wearing the same clothes as that morning in Delverton's office. Her reaction confirmed my suspicions that she'd been the woman who'd fled from there.

Her rueful smile acknowledged that the game was up. "You were in Tony's office this morning," she admitted.

"I saw you before that, too," I replied. "Although I don't think you saw me. You called into the hotel where he was staying in Paxham. I was staying there too."

Billy looked confused, frowning at each of us in turn. "Val? Aidan? What's going on? Do you two know one another, then?"

"We've never been introduced," I said. "But if you sit down, Billy, I'll try to explain. Perhaps with a little help from Miss Kaye?"

Valerie Kaye nodded, her gaze fixed on me. She couldn't know what was coming, and I was relieved she'd remained in her seat, willing to give me a hearing. Billy plumped down next to her, puzzled.

I began by asking Valerie to bear with me for a moment, as I needed to give them both some background relating to past events which had some bearing on the present situation. Billy indicated that he'd told Valerie a few days earlier about his sister's death from an accident on the cliffs beyond Paxham.

"Connie had known, from her time as a district nurse," I went on, "a small boy named Georgie Kell, who died in the Paxham ferry tragedy more than twenty years ago. There've always been rumours, although now they're gathering pace, that it was Edward Hambling who died, and that Georgie was brought up as Edward. Edward's paternal grandfather is General Marcus Hambling. He's in a Sussex nursing home and not in a good way. Edward's his sole heir." I paused to see that they were both watching me intently. "Connie called on General Hambling at the same time as Tony Delverton, and she recognised him when he showed up in Paxham. Tony was visiting the general to ask for money to help out the widow of Hambling's other son, who was killed in the war. He said she was his sister."

Valerie Kaye was shaking her head. "Tony was abandoned by his mother at birth and brought up by Barnardo's. He never had a sister."

"After your meeting with him in Paxham," I added, "he told us that *you* were his sister."

She sighed wearily. "I'm not his sister. I was actually something far worse than that."

The mood in the room had expanded into a singalong, with the man in the bowler raucous at the piano. Billy was straining to hear what was being said, and Valerie could scarcely make herself heard.

"If we're going to get on to Tony," she suggested, "it could be a long night. Would you mind if we went somewhere quieter?"

133

Billy immediately suggested Fratelli's in Tower Bridge Road. He'd stand us all a fish-and-chip supper. As Valerie collected up her things and wrapped a shawl around her shoulders, Billy told me that he felt both confused and intrigued.

"It'll become clearer," I assured him. "You'll see." He rewarded me with a doubtful nod.

We walked out into the cool night air: it had been noisy and stifling in the function room. Valerie took Billy's proffered arm, and I walked along behind them. I had to suppress a smile: in her high heels, she was over a head taller than him.

Fratelli's was an unpretentious little takeaway and restaurant, and Billy was well known there. It was late, and there were few other diners. Over plates of cod and chips and mugs of strong tea, Valerie Kaye took up her story.

"I was at the height of my career during the war years. Played all the big venues in London – those that were still standing – and toured with ENSA, like Billy, entertaining the troops here and overseas. It was all going well.

"Then I made two mistakes which changed my life. My first was Lieutenant Virgil Rousseau, US Marines. I fell hard for him, and he whisked me off to the States straight after the war. It didn't work out. He saw a glittering career for me as a cabaret singer, with him as manager pulling the financial strings. Well, my heart wasn't in America, and I never got established there. Once it dawned on Virgil that I wasn't going to be the pot of gold he'd anticipated, we divorced, and I returned to England. It was the early 1950s: the music, the singers, the mood were all different, and I struggled to take up where I'd left off. My star had waned, and I was down on my luck.

"It was a bad time to meet Tony Delverton. He was my second mistake. He was full of charm, had a bit of money – though I'm not sure where from – and comprehensively swept me off my feet. Gradually, I won back some confidence and, with Tony directing operations, started to get the engagements again. Nothing compared to the war years, but even so, I was earning decent money.

"Tony had done time early on, but he assured me he was on the straight and narrow. I was warned about him – his reputation went before him. But fool that I am, I decided to give him the benefit of the doubt. We married, and that put my hard-earned money under his control. He'd always have some project on the go, and it'd often border on the dubious. I'd 'lend' him money, and he'd never let on exactly what it was for.

"I was happy to be working and earning again. But as fast as I earned it, it'd get blown away on one of his dodgy schemes. And there were the women: something I'd been too busy to notice up to then. That signalled the end. We've been divorced six years but have remained in touch. The past two or three years have seen a number of his schemes backfire. I guess he was on his uppers, although he'd never have admitted it. Again, I was weak. He came to me, cap in hand, and I lent him money, to get him out of a hole.

"I had to draw the line. I was short of cash myself, but of course, he'd gone to ground. I called at the pub near his office, confident that they'd know him well. I played up to the landlord a bit, and he let on that Tony had gone down to Paxham. I suspected another of his schemes. I followed him there and demanded my money back. He had the barefaced cheek to ask for more!

"And now, I'll never get it back. The police called yesterday to tell me what had happened. It's typical that drink should have been the cause of it. I went to his office today, to see if there was anything I could salvage, but I only found a pile of unpaid bills. I'm sorry to have dashed off like I did. I had no right to be there and was worried that you might be one of his associates, or someone else he owed money to.

"You see, what you said about Tony trying to get money from this General Hambling – well, I'm sure he wouldn't have been operating alone. He was involved with some barmaid – huh, when was there not a barmaid? – and I think he might have hatched some scheme with her."

I hoped I'd put on a brave face. *Holly again.* My mind was racing: how on earth could she have got involved with the likes of Delverton? *"She'd been down on her luck a bit,"* Olive at the Nine Bells had said. Had Delverton helped her, but at a price? Because there'd always be a price where his type was concerned. And then she'd come to loathe him? Enough to wait in hiding for him the other night and shove him off the quay? But no – *no*, I couldn't believe that of her...

I forced myself back to the here and now, expecting both Valerie and Billy to be staring at me questioningly. But in fact he was staring at her. She looked distracted, deep in thought.

Suddenly, she snapped out of it and grabbed at my arm. "You know, it's only just come back to me, your mentioning this General Hambling. I *thought* his name rang a bell." She turned towards Billy. "Remember the old Elysium?"

"Do I *remember*?" Billy laughed. "How could any of us forget it? What times we had there during the war. Just off the Strand, wasn't it? Blimey, Val, that place was always packed to bursting."

"Yes, it was. And General Hambling – Aidan mentioning the name's brought it all back to me. He came to the Elysium."

"What, to hear you sing? You had quite a few admirers among the military bigwigs."

"He was no admirer. He came to disrupt the performance and had a blazing row with his son, who'd just got married. Lots of bad language and flying fur. He disowned the son and insulted his new wife in front of everyone, before storming out. Poor kid, she was one of my backing singers, my Larkettes. I can't recall her name, because they came and went so quickly. My, she was absolutely distraught."

Billy had turned pale and was staring at me open-mouthed. "Con was *there!*" he gasped.

"Your *sister?*" Valerie looked at him in disbelief. "Didn't you say she was a district nurse? What was she doing in a place like the Elysium?"

"Looking for me!" Billy's cry was so loud that the other diners all swung round to stare at him. He held up a hand in apology. "It was the day after one of our old relatives had died," he went on more quietly. "Con was searching all over for me to tell me the news – the funeral was the next day. She couldn't find me anywhere – think I was somewhere with a young lady. She told me later about the general and the bad language – she never held with that sort of thing. And my, didn't she give me an ear-bashing when she finally caught up with me!"

I sat stunned. Connie had been present when Hambling had disowned his younger son!

Then might she have died because she recognised a face from the past?

31

We finished supper, and I thanked Valerie for telling us all she had. She believed her ex-husband's death had been a tragic accident, and I didn't suggest otherwise. Privately, I wasn't so sure.

"Life wasn't easy with Tony around," she said, dabbing at her tears. "But I wouldn't have wanted it to end for him the way it did."

"I hope you get your career back on track," I said. "I saw the great pleasure you gave your audience this evening."

"The old songs and tunes'll never die," she smiled back. "They bring back so many memories, help us remember those who don't deserve to be forgotten."

I exchanged addresses with Valerie and promised to let her know how things turned out. She lived south of the river, and Billy hailed a taxi to take her home. "What a woman." He shook his head fondly, as we watched her being driven away. "She deserves better."

"She's got you as a friend, Billy," I told him. "I'm sure she's grateful for that."

With a broad grin, Billy clapped me on the shoulder, and we headed back to his apartment. Over more tea for me and a generous slug of scotch for my host, we discussed matters further.

I'd given a lot of thought to what I'd found out over the last few days.

"How did Connie get to know one of General Hambling's relatives?" I asked. "It has to have been the younger son, the one the general disowned when he stormed into the Elysium. Perhaps, after all, he survived the war? I know that Connie kept busy in retirement. Any ideas where she might have run into him?"

Billy polished off his scotch, brow furrowed in thought. "As far as I can tell," he said, "her time was divided between her chapel in Barber Street and the Seamen's Haven, where she helped out."

"Oh, where's that?"

"Not far away from here, in Rotherhithe. She'd go there often, along with a couple of others from the chapel. She was a qualified nurse, of course, and could help them with their minor ailments. She'd take Bible studies, listen to their troubles, pray for their souls, you name it. I'll take you along there in the morning." He frowned, eyes narrowing in suspicion. "Aidan, do you think Con – well, do you think she might have found out something she shouldn't?"

"I don't know, Billy. I didn't know her well, but she struck me as being a careful lady and an experienced walker. I can't believe she'd have wandered so close to the edge of that cliff."

"You don't reckon someone might have pushed her?" His voice was a tense whisper.

I looked back at him steadily. "It's no more than a suspicion," I replied. Although it was one I'd had for quite some time. "But I believe she knew something – something which was very important in the scheme of things."

Her words came back at me again. *"Surely – not the two of them?"* When she'd spoken them, apart from the ladies, Delverton and me, Holly had been the only other person in the room. *Had Connie been looking at her?*

"Might it have been about this lad Georgie Kell?" Billy suggested.

"Maybe."

Yes – maybe. I found myself grateful for the distraction. Connie had never got to meet Edward Hambling. Had she done so, might she have recognised the features of little Georgie? Had Georgie taken Edward's place? Because Edward alone could claim the general's legacy and bring about the restoration of Paxham Manor.

Then another thought turned my mind in a different direction. The Georgie/Edward rumours had been buzzing round the village for years. Yet it was only in recent weeks that they'd gathered pace; only recently that they'd started to really get at Edward, to eat away at him.

I asked myself why that should be happening *now?* And who might stand to gain from them? And – if indeed he was still alive – where did Freddie, the general's younger son, fit in?

Because Freddie had, just in the past few hours, suddenly leapt into the equation. And the suspicion was forming in my overworked brain, that what I'd read as the mystery might not actually be the mystery at all.

That I'd been approaching the whole matter *from entirely the wrong angle.*

I stared back at Billy. I'd said it myself: *no more than a suspicion.* I didn't want to force my fears on to him at this stage. As for my anxiety over Holly, that hadn't diminished in the least.

We went to the Seamen's Haven straight after breakfast. The previous day's exertions meant that I'd slept well. But my dilemma remained. I was determined to see this through as a debt to Connie; while Holly's involvement filled me with foreboding. But I couldn't back off now.

The Seamen's Haven was a Victorian warehouse on the waterfront, converted into a hostel for retired and homeless ex-sailors. Billy had met Reg, the warden, at Connie's funeral, and the two men had struck up an acquaintance.

Reg, a wiry, former featherweight boxer in his fifties, took us to his tiny office and poured tea into huge, cracked mugs. "We shall really miss Connie," he told me. "She cared very deeply for the men who passed our way."

"Was she especially close to anyone?" I asked.

He smiled wearily. "She'd do what she could. Particularly for those who had nothing. There was a sad case recently, and she desperately wanted to get something sorted for him. He had a heart condition, see, and an operation might have made all the difference. But he was penniless, and it was way beyond ours and Connie's means.

"Last time I saw her, though, she was fired up about it, reckoned she might have an idea how the money could be raised. She went away for a few days, but this poor chap went rapidly downhill and died, and, of course, we had no way of contacting her."

Another angle. I was back with my thoughts of the previous evening.

"This man wouldn't by any chance have been called Freddie Hambling?" I asked tensely, realising I had all Billy's attention.

Reg shook his head. "We only knew him as Wilf. He never gave a second name. Told us he didn't have one." He frowned. "But then, if his name was Wilfred, maybe at some stage he'd preferred to be known as 'Freddie', rather than 'Wilf.'"

Billy and I exchanged glances. Another piece of the puzzle had just clicked into place. I recalled Connie's last words: she'd said 'Wilf', not 'Will'. *Poor Wilf.*

"He'd been living rough for a long time," Reg went on. "By the time he ended up here, he was a sick man. It took Connie a deal of time to win his confidence, but she stuck at it. Patience of a saint, that sister of yours, Bill."

139

"She had that," Billy confirmed. I saw his lip tremble. But I noticed something apart from sadness: the beginnings of anger. Billy no longer thought his sister's death had been an accident. Someone had been responsible for it, and he intended finding out who that was. I felt I should be on my guard, for Billy's sake.

"Turned out Wilf was an ex-sailor," Reg went on. "Out in the Med during the war, and his ship got torpedoed. He was lucky to survive. Clung on to some wreckage and got washed ashore on this Greek island. An old couple took him in and nursed him until he was well again. He settled there, helped run their smallholding. But they died, a son turned up from nowhere to claim it, and Wilf was left with nothing. He spent what money he had on returning to England, but things went from bad to worse. His wife had given him up for dead and moved on. He wasn't able to track her down, believed she'd either remarried or died. And his father had disowned him: the hard-hearted so-and-so turned him away from his door.

"So, Wilf became a gentleman of the road, until he got sick and showed up here. He always hoped he might meet his wife again, had an old photo that he'd carried with him all those years. Connie promised she'd try to track her down."

"Then *he* gave her the photo?" I suddenly saw where this was heading, and Reg looked surprised at the note of urgency in my question.

"Well, yes, I s'pose he did. It certainly wasn't among his effects. Why? Is it important?"

"His *wife. Wilf's wife.*" The others were looking at me oddly, and I decided I'd better enlighten them. "Billy, cast your mind back. When PC Curtis handed back Connie's handbag, did it contain a photograph?"

Billy looked bemused. "No, lad. Definitely no photograph."

And yet, I'd picked one up and handed it back to her, when Connie had dropped her handbag in the lounge at Harbour Heights.

Which meant that someone had taken it.

Reg gave us a few more details, but nothing we didn't already know. He concluded that, in his opinion, Wilf's wife was probably dead.

But I couldn't help wondering if she might not be very much alive.

32

We thanked Reg and returned to Billy's apartment. Billy said little on the walk back, his expression grave. I told him I had to return to Paxham. That lit the fuse.

"You're not going without me, lad. There's been some funny business. You've been thinking along those lines for a while, and you've got me thinking the same. Poor Con never harmed a soul in her whole life. Now she's been done to death and, hang it all, boy, I want to see somebody brought to account over this. I'm coming with you."

I didn't want him there and had to say so plainly. I had questions I needed to ask, and while the clues had turned up outside the village, I was sure the solution to the mystery lay in Paxham itself.

And that Holly was part of it...

Things were getting so heated, that in the end I had to confide that much to him. I hadn't wanted to and, having done so, realised I'd been trying not to admit it to myself. But once I'd shared it with him, Billy climbed down and apologised. I promised I'd phone him the following day, but he quickly countered that by saying that, if he'd not heard from me by early next evening, he'd be on the first train to Paxham.

We parted on friendly terms, and I bundled up my things to head for the station. I phoned Harbour Heights from there. Billy would have let me phone from the apartment, but I preferred the privacy of the telephone kiosk, despite its stale, smoky atmosphere.

Holly answered. "Aidan! Hi! Are you on your way back?"

I tried to sound casual but felt she'd guessed that something was wrong. I told her that I was about to board the train and should arrive in Paxham at around four-thirty.

"Then I'll meet you at the station."

"I'm really looking forward to seeing you, Holly. But, well, we need to talk..."

She suddenly sounded subdued, almost meek. "Yes, Aidan, of course. I-I'll be there. See you later."

As I set down the receiver, I thought that she must know what I was going to say, and my gloom deepened. The black mood engulfed me for the whole journey.

But she was waiting at Paxham station, as she'd promised, trim and smiling in her yellow dress. In my misery, I'd half-expected her not to show up, and yet it was with no feeling of relief that I took her in my arms and kissed her. She must have realised that I was on edge, for I could sense anxiety in her searching gaze, as we drew apart.

I slung my duffel bag over my shoulder and, with her hand resting tenuously in mine, left the station and started off towards the village. Our recalcitrant gazes met at the same moment, and we stuttered to a halt.

"Wh-what's wrong, Aidan?"

But I could tell from the fear in her eyes, the way they couldn't quite meet mine, that she already knew. I so badly wanted to let her down gently, to show that I understood and was firmly on her side. But my throat felt dry, and it took such effort to squeeze out the words, which sounded harsh and accusing to my own ears.

"Holly, I – I found the pub, the Nine Bells, where you worked. It – it's close to his – Delverton's – office..."

She couldn't look at me, and I barely caught her reply. "Yes. I knew him."

"Why didn't you say? You could have told me, Holly. I'd have understood."

The words tailed away into a long silence. She was staring at the ground and even when, finally, she dragged her gaze up, she was unable to look at me. As I stood awaiting her reply, I had never felt so helpless, so inadequate.

"Because I couldn't. Just – just couldn't. Oh, Aidan, I'm so sorry about all this. I know I should have trusted you. I wanted to, believe me. But – well – I-I'm so ashamed. You see, I'm not what you think, nothing like what you think. I wish I could tell you more but I – I simply can't. It'd be for the best if you had nothing more to do with me. I'm not worth it. Please, *please*, go back home and forget you ever met me..."

She broke away in tears and ran off towards the hotel. Distraught, I called after her to come back, but in vain. She rounded the street corner, and I could hear the anguished slap of her sandals on the pavement, as she distanced herself from me.

I made my gloomy way back to Harbour Heights, where Eleanor Neale welcomed me. There was no sign of Holly, and I was sure Eleanor must have put two and two together; but fortunately, she made no comment.

There were four other guests staying that evening, and Holly served dinner. She remained polite and detached with them but avoided eye contact with me and didn't speak.

She wasn't in evidence later that evening, when Eleanor informed me that she'd received a call from Irene Pake, informing her that General Hambling had passed away earlier in the day, as the result of a heart attack.

"Irene sounded her usual bitter self about it. Just what her ladyship was counting on, she said, and I couldn't but agree. She'll be queening it over the whole village more than ever, the minute they've got their hands on the general's money."

I asked if Holly might have gone up to the Manor to offer her condolences, but Eleanor told me she'd done the washing up and gone straight to her room. Her sympathetic smile, as she handed me my key and I departed upstairs, told me that she knew something was very wrong.

It would turn out to be far worse than she might have imagined.

33

There was no sign of Holly when I went down to breakfast the next morning. The four new guests were already in the dining room, and Eleanor was flitting busily between there and the kitchen. However, as soon as she caught sight of me, she set her tray down on the reception desk and faced me, arms folded and expression stern.

"Now look here, Aidan. I don't know what's going on with you and Holly, but if you'll take my advice, you should kiss and make up, the pair of you. I've no idea why a girl like her would be interested in someone like Edward Hambling. Him and his stuck-up grandma treat her like a skivvy, and they'll want nothing more to do with her now the general's gone and they'll have his money."

Taken aback by Eleanor's unwonted use of my Christian name, I heard her out – there was no alternative – and came to a decision. I'd take Holly aside and implore her to let me into her confidence. I'd promise to do all I could to help her, no matter how deeply she might be involved.

I thanked Eleanor for her concern, because her lecture had been kindly meant. "Then, where is she?" I asked. "I really need to speak to her."

Eleanor shrugged huffily. "Goodness only knows. Somebody phoned, practically the minute we got downstairs. Holly took the call, told me it was urgent and would I excuse her? Huh, couldn't do much else. She was halfway out the door by then and looking as pale as a ghost."

"Do you know who phoned?"

"She never said. Promised she wouldn't be long. Mind you, that was an hour ago. I expected her back before now."

I went into the dining room, deep in thought, determined to concentrate my efforts on finding Holly. I summoned up some dregs of politeness and exchanged good mornings and weather observations with the two couples, who were halfway through their breakfast. They were on their way down to Cornwall, and once they'd finished, gathered their things, settled up and left. I took my empty plate and cup through to the kitchen. Eleanor came out to meet me, looking perplexed. "Still no sign of her," she said.

I was about to reply, when I was interrupted by a shrill cry from the doorway. "Ah, Miss Neale! I want you!"

Eleanor set down my crockery and turned, affronted, as Ruth Bayldon strode purposefully up to the reception desk. In windcheater and mannish-looking hat, she looked more formidable than ever and certainly meant business.

"*Where* is Edward?" she demanded.

Eleanor stared back coolly. "I'm sure I have no idea, Mrs Bayldon."

"He's not here with that girl, is he? I've noticed the sly looks he's been giving her recently."

"She's not here herself," came the blunt reply.

"I do hope you're not fencing with me," Ruth Bayldon snapped. "As the girl's employer, you must surely have some idea where she is?"

144

"I have *no* idea, Mrs Bayldon." Eleanor sounded as if she was spitting nails. "All I can tell you is that neither Holly nor Edward are here. I'd have you know that I was brought up strict chapel and that I'd countenance nothing improper going on under *my* roof."

Ruth Bayldon stared at her for a full twenty seconds, and Eleanor gave it back. It was Ruth who buckled, letting out an anguished sigh.

"Forgive me, Miss Neale. I'm not myself this morning. I awoke abruptly, found Edward gone, and I've simply no idea where he's gone or why."

The apology was acknowledged with a stiff nod. "Come through to the lounge and sit down."

I offered to make us all some tea.

"Good idea, Aidan," Eleanor said. "Nice and strong. I think we all need it."

She was sitting across from a worried-looking Ruth Bayldon, as I came in and set the mugs before them. Ruth looked up bleakly and nodded her thanks.

"Edward received a phone call late last night," she said. "He was most evasive when I asked him who'd called and tried to pass it off as the parent of one of his pupils. I know that wasn't the case. He was on edge for the rest of the evening, and when I awoke this morning, he'd gone. His bed hadn't been slept in, and I believe he must have slipped out in the early hours." She paused, looking helpless and anxious, as she cast us both a pleading glance. "I'm concerned about his mental state," she went on. "He's seemed so low of late, barely scraping a living with his teaching and becoming increasingly irritable. I'd much rather he didn't become attracted to that girl. He can do better than that."

A little of her customary fire blazed back in those last words. Eleanor seemed about to take umbrage, so I stepped in smartly.

"Surely, yesterday's news is likely to ease some of the pressure on him," I said. "And as for Holly, she's only trying to help. Edward needs friendship."

"Yes, yes, of course." Ruth was impatient, dashing that aside. "As for dear General Hambling, it wasn't unexpected." Her fractious gaze switched to Eleanor. "The news of his passing has spread around the village with indecent swiftness. The Pake woman, I dare say. She's always had a massive chip on her shoulder and delights in malicious gossip." From her look, she was bracketing Eleanor with Irene Pake, sweeping

145

on before Eleanor could react. "But there's also been the business of that wretched man Delverton. How *could* Curtis even begin to think that Edward might be involved? It continues to hang over him like a curse."

Eleanor and I exchanged meaningful glances. "Anyway, Mrs Bayldon," she said, "at this precise moment, we don't know where Holly is either. I was saying to Aidan here that she took a phone call first thing and off she went.

"From whom?" Ruth demanded.

"We don't know," I cut in, aware that Eleanor was about to bridle again. "Possibly she and Edward have met up somewhere. I'm as concerned as you are and intend looking around Edward's usual haunts."

"Oh, Mr Verney, would you?" Ruth positively gushed, almost breaking out in a smile. "You're most kind."

"But I think you should inform PC Curtis," I added.

"Oh, I agree. And if I can't shake him into action, I shall telephone the Chief Constable." She finished her tea and slammed down the mug with a sense of purpose. "Well, thank you, both. Do please keep me informed."

She arose and swept off without further ado. Eleanor watched her go with cynical detachment.

"Poor old Bob Curtis. I don't reckon he'd be wanting to organise a search party just yet. Not that her ladyship'll give him any choice. Huh! Chief Constable indeed!" She caught my frown. "What's wrong?" she asked.

"Something, Miss Neale. But I'm not sure what." I didn't add that I felt it was all linked together.

I told Eleanor I'd head for St Audric's chapel on the coastal path: it was Edward's favourite bolt hole. After a bright start, the morning was now overcast, with a stiff breeze blowing in off the sea, and the climb was a tiring one. Once there, I searched among the ruins but found no trace of the missing pair.

I called in at Harbour Heights on my way back, but Eleanor had nothing to report. I said I'd continue looking and went on to the Lobster Pot.

Bet Parrish was behind the bar, left in sole charge, as Irene had gone to the brewery in Leesbourne. "She only told me as we were closing up last night. Hope she makes it back by lunchtime, or I'll be rushed off my feet."

Clarence Darby had just arrived. I greeted him and asked if he'd seen anything of Edward and Holly.

He hadn't; but Bet said she had.

"Edward came in here, only minutes after I'd opened up." She looked at the clock above the bar. "Not far off two hours ago."

"Holly wasn't with him?"

"Not seen her since yesterday. Tell you what, though, lovey, Edward really shocked me. Lumbered in looking like death warmed up and asked for a *large whisky,* if ever you did. Doubt if he'd had one before in his entire life. I asked if he was all right, and he mumbled that he'd just had a row with someone. He downed his drink real quick, slammed down the glass and hurried off."

I'd grown increasingly anxious with every word Bet had uttered. I was about to press her for more, when the door yawned back, and Snowy Neale trudged in. His head was bowed, his face pale, and there was little trace of his usual affability.

"Someone looks like he needs cheering up," Bet remarked, as she pulled a pint of mild and set it before him. "Here, Snowy, Aidan's looking for Holly and Edward. Seems they've lit off without telling anyone. That'll make some juicy gossip for Irene to get her teeth into."

"Well, I've seen 'em." Snowy's reply was almost grudging. "A few hours back, though. Soon after I'd made harbour with the morning's catch. There was a couple walking up the lane past the cottages, and I'm sure it was them. The lass seemed to be trying to reason with him and not getting very far. Reg'lar down in the dumps, he was."

"Up the lane?" I asked. "Heading away from Paxham?"

Snowy nodded. "Up towards Barrowfield and the main road," he confirmed. "Everything all right, Aidan?"

"I just need to find them." I was more worried than I cared to admit. Holly and Edward had been seen together, and then, two or three hours later, Edward had appeared in the Lobster Pot alone...

I thanked Snowy and Bet and, on my way out, said goodbye to Clarence Darby. He barely acknowledged me, staring distractedly into his glass of wine. Everyone seemed out of sorts today.

The lane wound up past several rows of cottages, which I recalled from my visit to Snowy the other day, through an area of woodland to continue parallel to the estuary, as it climbed for two or three miles before reaching the main road. I stopped various people along the way, as well as inquiring of several out tending their gardens, if they'd seen a girl and young man that morning. I gave brief descriptions but drew a complete blank.

I was feeling increasingly desperate and in need of rest and refreshment by the time I reached Barrowfield, a village straddling the main road from Leesbourne. The pub was closed, but there was a teashop in the post office, and I had tea and a sandwich, repeating my inquiries with the waitress and postmistress. But to no avail.

By now, I felt sick with worry. I didn't for a moment believe that Holly and Edward might have run off together. Indeed, why should Edward want anything to do with her, when he was about to inherit his grandfather's wealth?

And why had Holly been trying to get close to Edward? Had he objected to this, and it was the reason for the altercation between them, which Snowy had witnessed? What if the quarrel had been so bad that he'd assaulted the girl or, worse, killed her? I'd witnessed Edward's ungovernable rage with Delverton only the other day.

I paid for my snack and headed back the way I'd come, picking up my pace, as it occurred to me that Eleanor and Ruth Bayldon might well be waiting on my report. As I came out from the wooded area and alongside the first row of houses, I heard someone call my name. Looking up, I saw Clarence Darby seated on the veranda of a small bungalow and went over to meet him.

"Muggy sort of day for a walk," he remarked. "And you look as though you may have been walking since I saw you in the Lobster around lunchtime."

"Yes," I replied. "I feel as if I've covered a few miles."

"Then take the weight off your feet, and I'll fetch us some lemon tea."

Clarence indicated an armchair, waited until I was installed, then left his own rocker and disappeared into the bungalow. I leaned back and closed my eyes. I must have dozed, because the next I knew, there was a steaming beaker on the table before me, and Clarence was back in his own chair.

"Oh, I – I'm sorry," I apologised.

He dismissed it with a kindly grin. "You've clearly walked some distance, young man. I heard you talking to Bet and Snowy earlier. Did you find any trace of your friends?"

I shook my head. "I went as far as Barrowfield, asking there and along the way. I'm very worried, Mr Darby. If they came this way together early on, and Edward showed up at the pub soon after eleven, what can have happened to Holly?"

He stared thoughtfully into his tea. "I don't sleep much these nights and am usually up with the lark. It was a fine morning early on, I sat out here, read and took a leisurely breakfast.

"Young man, I think Snowy was mistaken. I'm almost one hundred per cent certain that they didn't pass here, and this lane is the only way up to the main road. I recommend that you speak to Snowy again."

I finished my tea and thanked Clarence. I needed to return to Harbour Heights, in case Eleanor had news, before seeking out her brother. Clarence promised to phone Eleanor and inform her that I was on my way.

The lemon tea, the short rest and my increased perplexity on account of Clarence's information spurred me on, and I strode off down the lane. Within five minutes, I was in sight of the harbour. Checking my watch, I saw it was around opening time and wondered if I'd catch Snowy taking an early bevy in the Lobster Pot.

Except that I didn't have to go that far.

He was coming out of a cottage near the foot of the lane, and it wasn't his own. I made to hail him but thought better of it. Snowy was less than twenty yards distant, and there was a furtive air about him as he locked the door and shambled down the front path. He turned to latch the gate and looked around.

I'd had the foresight to crouch down behind a low wall. When, finally, I peeped over it, he was walking off towards the harbour, and it was safe to come out of hiding.

As I drew level with the cottage he'd just left, I recalled Snowy telling me that Annie Midson had lived 'in the next row up the lane' from him. It occurred to me that

149

this must have been the one he meant. And what had he been doing there, for he'd had a key? I decided to take a closer look.

I crept down a side passage, which took me round to the back of the row. Locating the cottage Snowy had just vacated, I listened intently but heard nothing. The curtains were drawn, and it appeared no-one was in. However, the kitchen window obligingly stood a few inches open.

Taking a cautious look around, I opened it as wide as I could and scrambled up over the sill. As I cleared the kitchen sink, my foot caught a plastic bottle of washing-up liquid. It thudded softly on the tiled floor, and I froze for several moments, listening, before stooping to pick it up. Still nothing.

The cottage was lived in, evidenced by the small fridge and stock of food in the pantry. I stole through to the next room, where the curtains were also drawn across. A door off to the right was locked, so I took a careful look around the room I was in, trying to get an idea of who might be living there.

On the mantel shelf, almost concealed behind a row of tiny brass ornaments, I saw a photograph. My heart leapt.

It was a monochrome snap, creased and crumpled by the years and the pockets which had carried it. I picked it up and stared in astonishment, as I recognised the face in the photograph.

I was so intent upon it, that I didn't hear the door behind me open and registered too late the creak of a floorboard. I'd half-turned, as something swished in the air and struck me on the side of the head. I winced with sudden pain, as the world turned black.

34

I had no idea of the time, when I awoke. The room was in complete darkness, and I couldn't read the dial on my watch. My head ached abominably, and I found it difficult to open my eyes. I groaned, as my cautious fingers traced a large lump at the base of my skull.

The noise I made had given rise to movement somewhere in the room, the soft tread of footsteps. Hands reached out, found my aching head and gently probed it:

soothing hands. I put up my own hand, caught one of them, our fingers entwining: a hand I'd held before. My next emotion was a surge of relief at the knowledge that she was alive.

And then the thought ambushed me. *What was she doing here? Surely – surely not?* "Holly..." My throat constricted, as I forced out her name.

"Aidan?" Her voice was a whisper. As my eyes flickered open, I found myself lying crumpled on a narrow bed. I made out her silhouetted figure, standing over then crouching beside me. "Are you all right? You weren't moving. I was afraid -?"

"Someone hit me from behind," I whispered back. "My head's bursting, but otherwise..." I'd been about to say I was okay but quickly realised that I wasn't, not in this predicament. I changed tack, and my next words wavered with apprehension. "Holly – why are you here?"

"We're both here," she replied. "I – I don't know what they intend doing with us."

"Both? You mean Edward?"

Her hand gently guided my face, so that I was looking across the dark room. I made out the silhouette of a bed across from mine and the shape of a body stretched out upon it.

I was suddenly fearful. "Is – is he all right?"

"I think he's been drugged to keep him quiet. He's stirred now and again. They must have lured him away from the Manor last night. They phoned me this morning and gave me no option. If I hadn't agreed to come, they'd have killed him."

She grasped my hand, clutched it firmly. Her body was trembling, and I could tell that she was crying. I scrambled up into a sitting position, drew her in and held her close. Despite the relentless thumping in my head, it felt good holding her.

"Don't cry, Holly," I whispered. "We'll get away from here. Edward too." As the words left my lips, I wondered just how possible that might be.

"I feel I've betrayed Edward," she groaned. "That I got him into this. I don't care about me. I deserve everything that's coming. But poor Edward – and you, Aidan, above all, you. Oh, I really didn't want you mixed up in this. I'm so, so sorry."

151

It was strange how her words brought me some relief. They helped me believe that, rather than being a conspirator, she'd been forced into this, whatever it was. I couldn't be entirely sure. But I had some inkling, because those words of Connie's had come back to me, from the time she'd seen Delverton in the lounge at Harbour Heights. I felt sure they'd recognised one another.

'The two of them.' And now I knew the identity of the other.

I pulled her closer into me, tried to reassure her that everything would work out, tried to inject some conviction into my words, even though I felt entirely without hope.

At least I succeeded in stemming the flow of her tears, enabling her to explain herself in a steadier voice.

"I knew her before, you see. I was, well, down on my luck, and she took me under her wing. She was kind at first, fixed me up with that job at the Nine Bells. She had it in mind, even then, what she was going to do. Once she'd laid her plans, she invited me down here, got me the job at Harbour Heights.

"She wanted me to get close to Edward, to be her eyes and ears around the Manor. The rumours have done the rounds of the village for years, that it was Georgie who survived and not Edward. She'd learned that General Hambling was very ill, that it was only a matter of time."

"She's Wilf's widow, isn't she?" I cut in. "Wilf – Freddie – the general's younger son, whom he disowned. I found her photograph outside on the mantel shelf. Wilf had given it to Connie Instow. He was in urgent need of a heart operation, and Connie hoped to help raise the money for it. She'd had no luck with General Hambling, so I believe she came here to see if Edward could persuade him to help out. Connie came across her by chance in Paxham, and I'd guess she pushed Connie over the cliff, because she didn't want her true identity revealed."

"I suppose she did," Holly sighed. "And she'd have played her part in stoking the rumours about the ferry tragedy. Her plan was for me to work on Edward. But that was where I had to draw the line. He was at such a low ebb and needed a friend. I was his lifeline to the real world, I suppose, even though he and his gran were suspicious of me.

"So, I'd done what she'd asked of me, keeping her informed about the state of the general's health. But now she wanted more: for Edward to be brought so low by the rumours that, when she staged his death, everyone would believe he'd taken his own life. I couldn't be a party to that. I didn't greatly like him; but I pitied him.

"Now, with the general dead, she'll have a claim on his money. She never remarried after Freddie went missing during the war. She knew General Hambling was wealthy, and I think she always had this in mind. And with Edward dead, she'd stand to inherit the lot."

There was a sudden movement from the other bed, but Edward must have been conscious for a while. He'd heard most, if not every word, of what Holly had said.

"You betrayed me." His voice was guttural with dismay and accusation. "Gran was right. I should never have trusted you. You weren't interested in me. And you and him – you both hate me. You're in this together."

"Edward, I'm sorry, I never meant -. And Aidan's got no part in any of this."

"Don't even speak to me."

Holly tried to remonstrate further, her tears returning, but she was silenced by the sound of a key turning in the lock. The door swung open, and light flooded the room. Snowy Neale stumbled in, his face drawn and shoulders hunched, looking every inch a beaten man.

Behind him in the doorway stood Bet Parrish.

35

Bet squeezed past Snowy, leaving him to guard the door. She looked around at three very anxious faces.

"Wh-what's going on?" Holly and I had the advantage over Edward because we knew. But he was totally bewildered. "What's happened? And why am I here with them?"

"You're a very important person, Edward," Bet informed him with malicious glee. "You're about to help put the last part of my plan into action. In fact, all three of you are." She stroked her chin thoughtfully, as she looked at each of us in turn. "I dare say it'll seen as something like this. You and Aidan quarrelled over her – not that she's worth it. She was playing each of you off against the other, and you weren't going to stand for it. You certainly showed another side to your character the other day, Edward. I never thought you had it in you, and that's a fact. And now no-one'll be surprised when you kill them both and top yourself out of remorse."

Holly was still clinging to my hand, as she faced Bet boldly. "You can't do it. He's suffered enough because of you. I – I won't let you."

Bet shook her head. Her mocking smile told me we could expect no mercy. "As if you're going to get a chance, lovey." She turned to Edward, who wouldn't look at any of us, his face turned away like a sulky child's. "I pulled her out of the gutter a couple of years back, Edward. Your snobby old gran'd have forty fits, if she knew what little Holly had had to do for a living."

Edward didn't reply. He shook his head wildly in an effort to dispel Bet's wounding words, covered his face with his hands. But she swept on relentlessly.

"I brought her down here to *spy* on you, sweetheart. Her job was to get to know you, throw herself at you, if need be. And she reported back everything you told her about your miserable old grandad. The closer he got to snuffing it, the happier I became. I went to him years ago, when my Freddie went missing and was reckoned to be dead. But he never gave me a penny, and me at the end of my tether. Blast him, who'd believe what I had to do to make ends meet. I swore then I'd have my revenge. And now that he's finally kicked off, this is the time. *My* time."

Snowy stirred wretchedly in the doorway. He'd been looking on in disbelief and now spoke for the first time. "Bet, you got to see reason. This has gone too far. You can't just get rid of 'em like that."

Bet's smile now was evil. "Oh, I reckon I can, Snowy my love. And I reckon you're going to help me. You're in this too deep to pull out now, particularly since you've already got one death to answer for."

Holly gasped, and everyone's gaze, including Edward's, turned to Snowy.

"Delverton attacked you!" he growled. "Ambushed you when you came out of the pub. If I hadn't been waiting there for you, he'd have throttled the life out of you. The man was out of his mind with drink. What did you expect me to do? Let him kill you?" He ran a hand over his anguished face. "Although now I'm wishing that maybe I had."

"But you didn't," she said bluntly. "And you're in this with me, Snowy, whether you like it or not. If they knew, people might not see it your way. Tony and I were lovers once, and when he hinted at it the other night, your face was a picture of jealousy. Quite a few of 'em in there noticed it. Oh no, Snowy my dear. You've got to go along with me right enough."

"Delverton was trying to get in on the act, wasn't he?" I was amazed at the steadiness of my own voice, amazed that I'd actually spoken, for I'd expected the shock of learning what awaited us would be enough to make the words stick in my throat. "He'd been down to Eastbourne, trying to con some money from the general. When that failed, he came here and tried to persuade you to let him in on the deal."

"I wasn't going to let *him* stand in my way," Bet threw back viciously. "I told him too much once, a long time ago, and he never forgot it. I thought I'd given him the slip when I came down here last autumn. But I'd sent a postcard to an old girlfriend of mine. Tony tracked her down and found out where I'd gone. And, yes, he wanted in. He was up to his ears in debt, and this was his last throw of the dice. Quite literally, as things turned out."

"Listen, Bet." Snowy looked and spoke like a desperate man. "We don't have to go this far. You never remarried, and as Freddie's widow you'd be entitled to something from the estate. You can work something out with Edward."

She stared at him in exasperation. "I wonder how a great lummox like you can be so soft," she sneered. "No, Snowy dear. Too much has happened. I've come so far now, and I want it all."

"And there are too many questions which haven't been answered," I followed up. "Such as Connie Instow. That old photograph on your mantel shelf out there: Wilf – Freddie – gave it to her. And when she came to Paxham to speak to Edward on Wilf's behalf, she recognised you from it."

Bet sniggered. "Don't know which of us was the most flustered," she said. "In she walked to the Lobster for her glass of lemonade and did a double take. I could almost hear her brain whirring as she looked at me. Then she dipped into her handbag, brought out this old photograph and studied it for what seemed like ages. She went and sat outside with her drink, and when I came out to clear away some empty glasses, she nabbed me. "This is an amazing coincidence, dear," she said. "But I really think this might be you." I pretended to look closely at the photo, then denied it. Admitted there was a similarity, but said I was confident it wasn't me.

"I could tell by the look on her face that she didn't believe me. Well, I couldn't afford for that photo to go the rounds; and I knew I had to do something about her. I could see from her gear that she was a keen walker. That made things a whole lot easier. The rumours were thick and fast by then, and there was some doubt over whether Edward really was who his gran said."

"And the rumours were making Edward increasingly distraught," I put in.

"Too true. That's why Miss Instow had to go. Besides, she'd known Georgie Kell, and she'd have recognised that Edward wasn't Georgie. So, I dared not let her meet him."

"She was a decent woman, trying to help someone in desperate need," I protested bitterly. "Don't you feel *any* remorse for what you've done?"

"Oh, spare me!" Bet cried. "I've slaved all my life behind bars, waitressing in cafés, getting groped by hideous old men and being treated like *dirt*. No-one's taking this away from me now."

Edward was shaking his head, probably still under the influence of whatever drug Bet had given him. She and Snowy must have had him in their clutches since the previous night. Bet's tale of Edward calling into the Lobster Pot that morning and Snowy's of having seen Edward and Holly together were clearly lies.

Holly, her face full of pity, reached for his hand to give what small comfort she could. But he shook her off, turned away, and she sank back defeated beside me.

"That's it, Edward," Bet sneered. "She's a common little cow, and she's got you into this. She'd have been no good for you. Here, Snowy, tie their wrists. It's past midnight, and no-one'll be around."

Snowy fetched some lengths of rope. He met no resistance from Edward. There was no spark in him at all, and I wondered if he understood what was about to happen.

I still held Holly's hand. Snowy parted us, but not roughly. He bound Holly's wrists, before calling over his shoulder to Bet.

"Better get that old jalopy of mine started," he said thickly. "It's a bit sluggish. I'll bring 'em out in a jiffy."

Bet nodded and went back through the house.

"Gimme your wrists, lad," Snowy ordered me sullenly.

I looked up at his harsh words. His tired eyes seemed to hold a message. He took hold of my wrists, pulled them behind my back and wound the rope round. Outside, the engine of Snowy's car sputtered into life.

"Keep 'em steady," Snowy snarled. I stared at him in astonishment. He'd only bound them loosely. He continued fiddling with the knots, bending to whisper in my ear. "This is for Annie. She was the only one, see, lad. *Always* the only one."

36

A car door slammed, and Bet came back into the room. She held a squat black gun and made sure we all saw it. "Another of Tony's side-lines," she said. "And it's not a toy, so don't get any ideas. Come on, all of you. Outside."

An old Ford Consul stood beyond the cottage gate. Bet checked that the lane was clear before, with Snowy bringing up the rear, she bundled the three of us into the back seat. Snowy drove, and she sat beside him, watching us closely; cold, committed.

She had little to worry about. Edward sat bolt upright, his posture reminiscent of his grandmother's. He stared straight ahead, but I doubted that he registered anything. He seemed almost catatonic, oblivious to what had passed or was about to happen. Holly's head rested on my shoulder. She didn't speak, but I could hear her softly weeping.

My mind was busy. Snowy's intention was for me to wriggle free from my bonds. But if I made a sudden dash for freedom, even supposing that I got away, the others would suffer. I had to consider them, await my moment. It couldn't be yet.

The journey was short. We'd driven up the lane beyond Paxham and turned down a bumpy track. We were heading towards the estuary, for I could make out the lights of Leesbourne, their reflection shimmering on the wide expanse of water.

The car juddered to a halt and Bet and Snowy got out and opened the doors. Snowy helped us out of the back, while Bet stood by, brandishing the gun as a reminder. A few yards away, the *Annie Mae* was moored at the water's edge, and I guessed we were a couple of miles downriver from Paxham harbour. I kept close watch on Bet, although she was alert to any threat we might pose. We were shepherded on to the boat, Edward silent and lacklustre, Holly with her head bowed, unable to look at any of us. Bet ordered us to sit on the floor in the stern.

Snowy started the engine, the noise exploding into the stillness. He steered the boat out into the middle of the estuary.

"Where are we going?" I asked.

"A nice, secluded spot down the coast," Bet said. "Not far."

Snowy turned from the wheel. "Bet, this is insane," he appealed. "They're three young people with their lives before 'em, gal. For pity's sake, let them go."

Bet's eyes flashed, and I caught a glimpse of her single-minded intent. There was going to be no way back for us.

"And give ourselves up, give up everything I've planned?" Her voice was a low, purposeful murmur, without a trace of mercy. "No, Snowy. We can't chicken out of it now."

Snowy's face was turned towards me, and I caught his barely perceptible nod. It was the signal, and I began to loosen my bonds. Holly, beside me, stared in amazement. I gave her arm a reassuring nudge with my shoulder.

Not that I could offer much reassurance. Snowy was still speaking, trying to talk Bet down, and she was arguing back, gesticulating with the gun to make her point. But he had all her attention.

Slowly, I got to my feet, crouched, steeled myself ready to spring. Then the boat lurched, knocking me off balance. Bet heard me, whirled round, the gun raised. My momentum had taken me to within a yard of her and, unable to point the gun, she swung it at me, clouting me on the side of the head. The force of it sent me sprawling on the deck, and I heard Holly scream, as Bet brought the gun round.

I caught a glimpse of Bet's face in the pale light from the wheelhouse: feral and full of menace. In that frozen moment, I saw my life ending. Strangely, I contemplated it with something like relief, putting an end to the worry and speculation of whether the cancer would return, how long I might have left.

But I'd reckoned without Snowy. The big fisherman had cut the engine and left the wheel. He spun the startled Bet round to face him and enveloped her in a bear hug.

She wriggled, yelled and swore, but he held her in a vice. As they teetered across the deck in agonisingly slow motion, the boat lurched again. Two muffled shots rang out, and I saw Snowy wince and close his eyes.

Squirm as she might in his grasp, Bet couldn't burst free. Grimacing as his strength ebbed away, Snowy hauled her across the deck and pitched them both over the side. I should never forget Bet's piercing, anguished scream before they hit the water.

As I staggered over, a torrent of spray spattered the deck, soaking us all. I peered over the side but saw no sign of them. Holly was beside me in tears, and I untied her wrists, did the same for the unresponsive Edward. I drew Holly into the wheelhouse and sat comforting her, as the boat drifted aimlessly down towards the sea.

I couldn't be sure how much longer we were on the boat. Everything seemed to pass in a blur. Edward's face was blank, staring at nothing in particular. I spoke to him and got no reply; although I couldn't remember what I'd said to him or Holly, as I held her tightly and we sat and waited.

Suddenly, it seemed, lights and voices erupted into the stillness. There was a lifeboat, many hands hauling us aboard; the reassuring face of PC Curtis. Someone took charge of the *Annie Mae,* and I saw a police launch combing the waters for some sign of Bet and Snowy.

A reception committee awaited us in the harbour, immense relief on every face. Eleanor and Clarence Darby were there; and, as I might have guessed, Billy Instow. He'd arrived at Harbour Heights earlier in the evening, as he'd threatened, when there'd been no phone call from me.

Clarence had phoned Eleanor soon after I'd left him, to tell her I was on my way back. When I didn't show up, she and Billy alerted PC Curtis, who'd already been in touch with his Leesbourne colleagues over the disappearances of Edward and Holly.

Later that evening, Clarence had called in at the Lobster Pot. He'd thought Bet looked distracted, and Snowy didn't put in an appearance, something almost unheard of. On his return home, Clarence learned from Eleanor that there was still no sign of me, so he contacted PC Curtis with his observations.

We all went back to Harbour Heights, where steaming mugs of cocoa were handed out. Ruth Bayldon had shown up at the harbour to reclaim Edward, and PC

Curtis had driven them home. Holly, exhausted, went to her room, leaving me to thank Eleanor, Clarence and Billy for their efforts.

Eleanor hugged me. "You're a brave lad, Aidan," she said.

"Not as brave as your brother," I replied. "He saved us all."

A tear rolled down her cheek. "Ah, brave but misguided. But he was a good man at heart, and the dear Lord in His mercy will take that into account, I'm sure."

37

It took all next day for matters to be settled. Holly, Edward and I spent several hours in separate interviews with PC Curtis and a detective inspector from Leesbourne CID. I'd warned Holly not to say too much about her involvement with Bet Parrish, although the inspector practically waved it aside. He and Curtis both felt that the girl had been used by the older woman, although only to gather information, and Holly swore that she'd had no idea that Bet had been responsible for Connie Instow's death, or that she'd intended to murder Edward.

I returned to Harbour Heights, certain that the rumours of the past twenty-one years had been nothing more than that. I believed that Colonel Bayldon, by all accounts a decent man, had had a soft spot for pretty Annie Midson; and that possibly he'd supplied her with some of the alcohol on which she'd become dependent, although with no sinister motive.

Bet Parrish, during her time in Paxham, had worked hard to stoke up the old rumours, in order to unhinge the vulnerable Edward. She'd found willing allies in Irene Pake and other villagers, who had no love for Ruth Bayldon.

Bet had also found a willing sidekick in Snowy Neale, festering with resentment over how Annie had lost everyone dear to her, and how that loss had led to her untimely death. However, I doubted that Snowy would have been party to the slow destruction of Edward Hambling.

By the following morning, I was, once more, the sole remaining guest at Harbour Heights, for Billy Instow had left for London by the first train. However, he'd extracted a promise that I'd visit him soon and, with a twinkle, extended the invitation to Holly. Then he'd enveloped the blushing Eleanor in a hug, before taking his leave.

Eleanor, Holly and I sat together over breakfast. I explained that I'd be heading home later that day. Eleanor put on a brave face over the loss of her brother, but we could see that she was devastated by his death and needed time to grieve alone.

"Always likely that a woman would be his downfall," she sighed resignedly. "How gullible he was, not to have seen through that evil Jezebel..."

We offered what consolation we could. Bet Parrish had been a scheming woman, able to mask her true character and ambition behind a friendly façade. Although, in my view, the situation had arisen out of General Hambling's monstrous stubbornness and arrogance. If only he might have found it in his heart to forgive his youngest son and have compassion for him in his illness...

Eleanor announced that she'd decided to sell Harbour Heights and move away. "There'll be too many memories here," she declared. "Besides, I'd like to see a bit more of the country while I'm able to get about easily. All I've ever known have been Paxham and Leesbourne, and it's about time I branched out. As well as owning his cottage, it transpires that our Jim bought Annie Midson's, not long after she died, and rented it out through an agent. So, with the sale of these properties, I shall have plenty to get by on."

Holly asked where she might go to begin with?

"Well, Mr Instow has very kindly offered to show me around London..."

She was blushing furiously again, and Holly and I, exchanging a meaningful glance, didn't press the issue. We assured her there was much to see in London and were sure she'd enjoy her visit.

Otherwise, Holly was subdued. That she and I hadn't had much to say to one another was a fact not lost on Eleanor. When Ruth Bayldon and Edward showed up a little later, Holly slipped quietly away.

Both were gracious in their thanks, commending me for my bravery in saving Edward's life. Ruth seemed less forbidding, her attitude no doubt mellowed by the reassurance of imminent money, and Edward's gratitude seemed sincere. As they were about to leave, I called him back and asked for a private word.

"I'm leaving Paxham this afternoon. Will you promise you'll make your peace with Holly? She's not proud of what she did, but she was forced to act against her will."

Edward shook his head adamantly. He remained forever stiff and formal. "I can't forgive her. She betrayed me to that woman, who intended to kill me. Also, Holly's past seems to have been, well, chequered to say the least. I've promised Gran I'll have nothing more to do with her. I can't be expected to turn a blind eye to the way she's treated me.

"Anyway, Grandfather's legacy means we can finally carry out some renovations to the Manor. Gran will expect much more of me now."

We shook hands and wished each other well. I watched him leave, trotting off up the road in the wake of his striding grandmother. I felt immensely sorry for him.

I went upstairs for my things, returned to reception for the last time and settled my bill with Eleanor. I asked where Holly was. I wanted to say goodbye but didn't feel I could insist, as I was unable to tell how things stood between us.

"Still in her room," came the glum reply. "She's taken this very hard. Talking about going back to London and finding work in a pub again."

I wrote down my home address and handed it over. "Ask her to get in touch." I was sure she noted the plea in my voice. "And Eleanor, please tell her she mustn't feel ashamed, not at all, and -"

Eleanor was back to looking her customary formidable self. "Oh, I know exactly what I'm going to tell her, Aidan. Now, what time's that train of yours?"

"Not till one-thirty. There's something I have to do first."

We embraced and promised to keep in touch. "Perhaps we'll meet up in London?" I suggested.

"We may well do, my dear. But anyway, meet up we certainly shall."

I left the hotel and headed for the little harbour chapel, where it had all begun for me on my first afternoon in Paxham, two weeks previously, when Connie Instow had walked in. I sat quietly before the memorial plaque and prayed for Connie and for us all. On my way out, I lit a candle and left it burning there, as I held in my heart the memory of a truly Christian woman, who'd only sought to help a man in desperate need, with no thought for herself.

And then I thought of General Hambling and Edward. It all came down, not only to forgiveness; but having the humility to forgive.

162

I was certain that Connie Instow would have forgiven them all.

*

She didn't arrive at the station. I'd been looking out for her, hoping she would. But the train came in, I boarded it, and as it pulled out, I took my long, last view of Paxham, that same view which had drawn me to it two weeks before.

I sought out a quiet compartment and settled down. I wondered what life might hold and realised I'd learned one thing. That I had to go on from day to day, to keep keeping on. I'd return home, try to find a job, forgive Diana, wish her well and consign her to the past.

As the train picked up speed, the compartment door slid back, and I sighed. I'd rather have been left alone with my thoughts. As soon as it occurred to me that the door hadn't closed, I looked up.

Holly stood there, a battered holdall in her hand. She looked dishevelled, her hair tousled, dress rumpled, face tearstained. I guessed she'd left Paxham in something of a hurry.

Or been kicked out.

"N-Nelly said I had to come after you, so I did. I'm just so ashamed of – of everything, and I can't expect you to forgive me or think well of me ever again. But – oh, Aidan, there's only you, you see – and please, *please,* don't send me away..."

I struggled to my feet, unsteady with the rocking of the train and faced her squarely.

"Send you away, Holly? I promise you I never shall."

I drew her in and sat her down beside me, took her hand in both of mine. The doctor's words came back to me. *"It may return. There can be no guarantees."*

My own thoughts overrode them: my thoughts and my will. I was done with the deceiving past. This was the here and now, the time to live.

We sat together for a long while in silence. When at last her face came up to meet mine, she was smiling.